They could see right through me.

"Lauren looks so silly holding Patrick's clipboard like she's in love with it," Ashley giggled.

Jodi laughed. I gave her a dirty look. She shrugged her shoulders. "Lighten up," she whispered to me. "I hate to agree with Ashley, but you looked like an ad for a movie: *Crush on the Coach.*"

Cindi giggled. I gave *her* a dirty look, too. "I do *not* have a crush on Patrick," I said.

"Your nose is growing, Pinocchio," whispered Cindi.

Look for these and other books
in THE GYMNASTS series:

THE GYMNASTS

#9 CRUSH ON THE COACH

Elizabeth Levy

AN
APPLE
PAPERBACK

SCHOLASTIC INC.
New York Toronto London Auckland Sydney

To the real Sixto Ulloa,
un político con mucho corazón.

ISBN 0-590-42821-7

12 11 10 9 8 7 6 5 4 3 2 1   0 1 2 3 4 5/9

Printed in the U.S.A.   28

First Scholastic printing, January 1990

I Like Gymnastics
More Than Politics

The day my picture was in the newspaper, I couldn't wait to get to gymnastics and be with my teammates, the Pinecones. I thought the gym might be one place where nobody would have read the Politics page.

My mom had decided to run for city council. Her picture was in the paper with her arms around me and my dad, and she looked terrific. I looked awful. The photographer had snapped us just as I was about to sneeze. I looked as if I had swallowed a worm. They might as well have put a caption under it: *Lauren Baca, Dork*.

Julia Baca Enters Race for City Council, read the headline. They didn't even mention me. But at school, the principal had made an announcement over the loudspeaker and put the picture up all over the halls. Mom has always loved politics. She's been wanting to run for public office for a long time. Finally she's getting her chance. Everyone says her opponent has been around too long. He can be beaten.

I've had my picture in the newspaper before. Once the Denver Zoo had a contest to name the new baby chimp. I picked Natasha, and Russian was "in." I got my picture taken with Natasha. Naturally, my best friend, Cindi Jockett, asked which was the chimp. Then it had been fun because it was just a one-time thing.

Mom picked Cindi and me up at school to drop us off at Patrick's. The official name of my gym is the Evergreen Gymnastics Academy, but everybody calls it "Patrick's" because he's our coach, and he's wonderful. Mom worries that maybe he's too young to be in charge, but I think he's terrific. And best of all, he likes me. Patrick laughs at my jokes, and he's told me I've got explosive power. In school, if a teacher told you that, you'd be in trouble. In gymnastics, it means you've got the potential to be great.

Cindi's the one who got me back into gymnastics. I had taken gymnastics when I was little, and then I had quit. I'm really glad Cindi talked me into coming back. I love it.

The backseat of the car was filled with boxes of leaflets that Mom was taking to her campaign headquarters.

Cindi jammed into the backseat. She took out one of the leaflets. " 'Baca's the Best. It's Time for a Change!' " Cindi read out loud. "I think this campaign is going to be neat."

I kept my mouth shut.

"Thanks, Cindi," said Mom. "I'll need your help to pass those leaflets around."

"You've got it," said Cindi excitedly.

I scrunched down next to the door in the front seat. Mom's campaign was threatening to take over my life. I didn't really have a right to complain. Mom had told me when she decided to run for city council that it might disrupt our lives. "Do it, Mom," I had told her. "I'll help."

But I didn't know what I was in for.

I was glad when we pulled into the road behind the Evergreen Mall, where our gym is. "Honey, try to be on time when you get out of gymnastics," Mom said to me. "I'm giving a speech on education late this afternoon. They're filming it for one of my TV commercials. Sixto thinks it'll look good if you are there to show I've got a child in the public schools." Sixto Ulloa is Mom's campaign manager, and lately he's been running our lives.

"You're going to have TV commercials? Neat!" exclaimed Cindi.

"It's not as glamorous as it sounds," said Mom. "It's just videotape, and we only have enough money to put them on cable TV, but I've gotten lucky. A filmmaker who works at the high school with Lauren's dad has volunteered, and he's really good."

"Maybe you can do an ad telling people that Lauren's a straight-A student," suggested Cindi.

"Don't be stupid," I muttered.

"That's not a bad idea, Cindi," said Mom.

I just groaned. It felt good to get out of Mom's car. I sprinted into the gym. Patrick greeted me with a big grin. He was standing next to the bulletin board where he keeps our schedule of meets and pins up articles about gymnastics or nutrition or even jokes.

"Hey, Lauren," he said. "I'm just putting up your picture."

I groaned again. I seemed to be doing that a lot lately.

"What's wrong?" Patrick asked. "I think it's great that your mom's running. She's got my

4

vote. I've never voted for someone I knew personally before. I think your mom is a terrific candidate."

I made a face. Patrick peered at me closely. "Aren't you excited about it?" he asked.

Before I could answer, the other gymnasts started arriving. Darlene looked at my picture up on the wall. "Hey, cool, Lauren," she said. "I didn't see that."

"Let me see," said Jodi, crowding in next to her.

"Me, too," piped up Ti An.

Becky Dyson was tall enough to see over Jodi's shoulder. "Lauren, you look like you swallowed a lemon. How come you're making such a stupid face?" Becky is the best gymnast at Patrick's and definitely the meanest. Luckily she's too good to be on my team.

The Pinecones are an intermediate group. Darlene Broderick is the oldest. She's thirteen, two years older than Cindi and me. I like her a lot. Darlene is beautiful, and her dad is famous. He's a football player with the Denver Broncos. You'd think with that combination Darlene would be stuck-up, but she's the opposite.

Jodi Sutton is eleven, too. Her mom is an assistant coach at Patrick's and you'd think Jodi would be a great gymnast, but she's not. She's not the best student in the world, either, but she's a lot of fun to be with.

Ti An and Ashley are the two youngest Pinecones. Ti An is eight and Ashley's nine. They're both tiny, but their personalities aren't anything alike. Ti An is sweet. She's shy, and I think she looks up to me. Maybe she likes me 'cause I'm short. I like Ti An.

Ashley is a different story. Ashley likes to think of herself as Little Miss Perfect. She is a perfect minus ten — zip for personality — zip for sportsmanship. Ashley thinks she's smart, but she really isn't. I think she's just plain spoiled. She always has to have the latest leotard, the most "in" gymnastics shoes. She's an only child like I am, but while my parents have bent over backwards *not* to spoil me, Ashley's parents give her everything she wants.

"Lauren, your face is all scrunched up," piped up Ashley as she stared at my picture. "How come?"

"I was about to sneeze," I muttered. I had had it with everybody crowding around my picture.

Luckily Patrick came to my rescue. "I think Lauren looks fine," he said. "However, I like her better up on the bars. Come on, guys. Enough of this. I posted the newspaper article because

I'm proud of Lauren and her mom, but let's forget about politics and get into the gym."

"Yippee!" I said. "I second that."

" 'Yippee'?" said Ashley. "Nobody says 'yippee' anymore."

Patrick ruffled my hair. "It's a proven fact that Lauren is an original," he said.

I grinned at him. Patrick knows that I always say "it's a proven fact." Well, it's a proven fact that I like gymnastics a lot more than politics.

A Real Joy

"I want to work on the bars today," said Patrick after we finished our warm-ups. "I want to work on our release moves."

"Can I be released from these moves?" I asked.

"Just for that, Lauren, I'll take you first," said Patrick.

"It's a proven fact that I should have kept my mouth shut," I whispered to Cindi.

I'm not very good on the uneven bars. I'm a good vaulter, but that's because it's over quickly. To be good at bars, you've got to be daring and consistent. Jodi's daring, but she's not consistent. Cindi's got the perfect personality for the bars; that's why she's so good at it. Cindi's got guts, and she works hard. She doesn't try anything stupid. Cindi can be spectacular on the bars. But not me. Besides, the bars scare me.

"Come on, Lauren," urged Patrick. "No excuses this time. I know you're ready for a release from the high bar."

"Aren't you supposed to get a release from her mom before she tries that?" joked Jodi. "It won't be good for Mrs. Baca's campaign if Lauren ends up splattered on the mats."

"That's not funny," I snapped.

Jodi blinked at me. "I was just kidding," she said.

Jodi knows that my parents aren't the biggest supporters of gymnastics in the world. They hadn't wanted me to start up again. They worry that gymnastics takes too much time away from my studies.

But I knew I shouldn't have snapped at Jodi. "I'm sorry," I muttered to her.

Jodi just shrugged and smiled. "No prob," she said. Jodi doesn't hold a grudge. I always know what she's thinking. If she's mad at me she lets me know. If she says "no prob," it means there's no prob.

Patrick explained what he wanted me to do. In

the middle of my routine, I was to grab the high bar. Then, when he said "go," I had to let go of the bar and swing around. I had done the turns before, but never completely letting go with both hands.

"You can do it," said Patrick. "And I'll be spotting you. As Jodi says, 'no prob.' "

"You sure I'm ready for this?" I asked Patrick.

"Trust me," said Patrick.

I did. I stood in front of Patrick and grabbed the lower bar. I pulled myself up and around.

"Right up to the high bar. Go, Lauren!" said Patrick.

I grunted. I could hear the bars creaking and groaning as I swung freely. Patrick grabbed my legs to give me support. "Don't worry. I've got you," he said.

I swung around the high bar into a handstand. I was breathing hard.

"Don't rest . . . don't rest," said Patrick. "Let go." I bit my lip as I released my grip on the high bar, making a 180-degree turn.

I would have fallen for sure, but Patrick held me steady. My heart was pounding. I couldn't believe I had let go of the bar and grabbed it again.

"Good girl! Good girl!" said Patrick as I made

my dismount. "That's the best you've done."

I beamed at him. "Let me try it again," I said. "I think I can do it better."

"It's my turn . . . my turn," whined Ashley.

Patrick smiled at me. "She's right. You'll get your chance again. But, Lauren, that was good . . . really good." Patrick gave me a thumbs-up sign. It meant more to me than the biggest bear hug in the world.

My hands were stinging from my workout on the bars. They were red and sore, but it was worth it. I couldn't wait to try it again, and that isn't like me at all on the uneven bars.

"You were good," said Cindi as I went to stand behind her in line. "Pretty soon you'll be competition for Becky."

"That'll be the day. First I've got to get good enough to beat *you*," I teased.

Cindi tossed back her long, curly, strawberry-blonde hair. "You'll keep me on my toes," she said.

I liked the idea of being real competition for Cindi. I always kind of thought of myself as standing in her shadow as a gymnast.

Patrick signaled for Cindi to approach the bars. Cindi was really exciting to watch. She almost seemed to float over the bars. She kept her body straight as a board during her giant circles. The bars shook and creaked and groaned with the force of her momentum, showing just how much power she was using.

"Awesome," I said when Cindi landed her dismount.

Patrick nodded his head. "Good work, Cindi," he said.

"Good work" is one of Patrick's highest terms of praise.

It was my turn again. "I'll never be as good as Cindi," I told Patrick as I grabbed the lower bar, getting ready for my mount.

"Lauren, you've made more improvement since you've been here than any kid I've coached. You've been a real joy. Now let's go to work."

Patrick's words rang in my ear: "A real joy."

I flung myself into my routine. I felt like a bird flying. I let go of the bar when I had plenty of height, and I knew that I had time to grab on again.

I wasn't afraid of anything.

I even nailed my dismount.

"Lauren," beamed Patrick, "that's the best workout I've seen you do. You're doing great!"

I was smiling so hard I felt like my face was going to break. I turned around and gave Patrick a hug. I was flying. Some days in gymnastics are so good. It seems as if there's no trick you can't do. Patrick says that gymnastics at its best is the closest humans will ever come to soaring. It's a proven fact that nothing — nothing — beats it. Honest.

3

Not My Favorite Activity

In the locker room, I was still high from my great workout. "Did you see my release move?" I bragged to anyone who would listen. I don't usually brag, but I felt so good.

"I can't do that yet," said Ti An.

"I didn't think I could," I admitted. "But Patrick just said do it, and I did it."

"Are you going to have your picture in the paper all the time now that your mom's running for city council?" asked Ashley.

I wanted to talk about gymnastics. "No," I said. "About my release move — "

"I saw your mom on TV last night on the news," interrupted Jodi.

"I saw a commercial for her on cable TV," said Darlene. "It made it all so real. It looked like a news program."

"That's because they have to use videotape," said Cindi, the new instant expert on Mom's campaign. "It's less expensive than film, and they can buy time cheap on cable. Mrs. Baca is going to have lots of different commercials."

It was hopeless. Everyone wanted to talk about Mom's campaign — everyone but me. "Since when do you watch the news, Jodi?" I asked, stripping off my leotard.

"Barking Barney was over for dinner," said Jodi. "He and Mom like to watch the news before dinner." Barking Barney owns a string of pet stores, and he's dating Jodi's mom.

"Is he going to vote for my mom?" I asked.

Jodi giggled. "He wasn't. But Mom and I argued with him. Don't worry. By the time of the election, we'll have him turned around. Maybe he'll do a commercial for your mom." Barking Barney's commercials are on the radio all the time. They always have a stupid pet joke.

"I wish kids could vote," said Ti An. "I'd vote for your mom."

"Thanks," I said, but I must have had an edge to my voice. Darlene picked it up. Darlene's very sensitive about what other people are thinking and feeling. She smiled at me. "It's kind of a drag, isn't it?"

"What's a drag?" asked Becky. She had a towel around her neck. She was drenched in sweat. One thing you had to say for Becky; she's nasty but she works hard.

"Having a famous parent," said Darlene.

"Oh puh-leeze," said Becky. "How can you compare Lauren's mom running for the dinky city council and your dad, a football star?"

"It's not a dinky job," argued Cindi. "It's a very big deal. Julia Baca could be mayor someday, maybe even President."

"Little Lauren in the White House? Spare me!" said Becky. "Lauren would probably invite Patrick to be her First Coach, private fitness instructor to the White House."

I giggled. "I like that idea," I admitted.

"Of course you do," said Becky sarcastically. "You've got such a crush on Patrick; you'd do anything for him."

"I do not have a crush on Patrick," I said.

"Yes, you do," said Cindi easily.

I stared at Cindi. I couldn't believe that she could see through me so easily. I guess I did have a crush on Patrick. Sometimes when I can't get to sleep at night, I daydream about Patrick and I getting kidnapped together and me saving his life. It's my favorite daydream, but I've never told anybody about it, not even Cindi, so how did she know I had a crush?

Becky laughed at me. "You should see your face," she said. "It's all red."

I stuck my tongue out at her. "Don't let the press snap your picture like that," warned Cindi.

Becky went into the shower. Cindi snapped her towel in the air. "Earth to Lauren . . . Earth to Lauren . . . are you there?"

I blinked my eyes. "Sure," I said, but I could feel I was still blushing.

Cindi looked a little guilty. "Sorry I said you had a crush on Patrick. I didn't mean to embarrass you. I think it's kind of cute the way you look up to him."

"That's just because I'm short," I argued. "It looks like I look up to him, just because he's so much taller than me."

Cindi laughed. "It's a proven fact. . . . Anyhow, forget about it. Want to come over to my house tonight? Jodi and Darlene are coming. We'll just hang out."

I looked at my watch. "I can't," I said. "Remember? Mom's picking me up. I have to go hear her speak at that rally."

"You're kidding!" exclaimed Darlene.

"Yeah, like you said. It's a drag. Almost every

evening and afternoon Mom's giving a speech somewhere, and lots of times I have to go."

"No, no," said Darlene. "I meant, you can't go dressed like that!"

I looked down at my clothes. I was wearing jeans and a Goofy T-shirt that I had gotten at Disney World last year. "Uh-oh," I giggled. "It's a meeting about education, and I forgot I wore my Goofy T-shirt. It's all I've got."

"Here," said Darlene quickly. "You like butterflies." She rummaged in her gym bag and came up with a perfectly folded purple T-shirt with a big butterfly on the front. It was huge, not just the butterfly but the T-shirt. It would come down to my knees.

"I'll swim in this," I argued.

"Put it on. I'll fix it," said Darlene. I put on the T-shirt. Darlene rolled up the sleeves and tied the bottom in a big knot. "You look adorable," she said. "The perfect candidate's daughter," she said.

I looked at myself in the mirror. "Maybe I should get Mom to hire you as my fashion consultant for the campaign," I said.

"I'll do it for free," said Darlene.

Jodi's mom stuck her head in the locker room. "Lauren, your mom's out front; she said to tell you to step on it."

18

I picked up my gym bag. "I still wish I were going to your house," I said to Cindi.

"Don't sweat it," said Cindi. "You won't miss anything. We're just going to hang out and have some munchies."

The problem was that hanging out and having munchies are two of my favorite activities. Going to a teachers' rally with my mom ranked maybe 342nd on my list of things I wanted to do.

4

There's a Tiger in My Stomach

Marilyn, the person in charge of Mom's media campaign, was sitting in the passenger seat in the front of our car, so I climbed into the back, pushing aside the cartons of literature.

"What is this place?" Marilyn asked, peering out the window at my gym with its creaky sign of an evergreen hanging over the door. There are gymnasts swinging from the branches of the tree, but the sign has already faded because of the winter storms.

Patrick's gym is at the end of an alleyway behind the mall. There's nothing around it except a few cottonwood trees and a dried-up stream. From the outside it does look like an old, abandoned warehouse. The first time I saw Patrick's, it reminded me of the place in TV movies where the bad guys always hung out to ambush the good guys.

"Patrick doesn't put money into the outside. He spends all his money getting us the best equipment," I said defensively.

"Hummmph," grunted Marilyn. She turned around in the seat and faced my mother, ignoring me. "Now, Julia, be careful this afternoon. I know how big you are on education, but don't promise more than you can deliver. We've got to get through to people that you're not just a big spender. Let me go through the six points of your speech."

"I had a great day in gymnastics," I told Mom.

"That's wonderful, dear," said Mom, but I knew she wasn't really listening to me. "We'll talk about it later. After the meeting, I'm taking this evening off. Your dad and I are having pizza with you, just the three of us."

"That'll be a treat," I said sarcastically.

"You *love* pizza," said Mom, sounding a little hurt.

I bit my lip. I hadn't meant to be nasty. It was just that I resented having to wait until after the meeting to eat. I was hungry now. It was already five o'clock.

I picked up one of Mom's "Baca's the Best. It's Time for a Change!" leaflets and started folding it. I love to do origami.

"Lauren, what are you doing?" Marilyn asked, turning around in the seat so she could peer over her shoulder at me.

"Making a good luck crane," I said.

Marilyn smiled, but it was a tight smile. "Please don't waste your mother's leaflets."

"You've got thousands of them," I argued.

Marilyn sighed. "And every one of them costs," she muttered.

"Thanks for the sentiment, though, honey," said Mom. "I can use all the good luck you can give me."

"Right," I mumbled. I put down my folded bird and sat with my hands on my lap. I tuned out whatever Mom and Marilyn were talking about and thought about Patrick and me. Patrick had called me a "real joy" to work with. I bet he would love it if I made him some origami good luck cranes.

Dad was waiting for us at the high school where the meeting was being held. He stood next to Sixto, Mom's campaign manager. Sixto's a short man, a little heavyset, but with a warm round face. He's got a smile for everyone. Mom says he's a great politician because he's so nice to people that they never suspect how competitive he really is. Sixto loves winning. He's not afraid to play hardball. You could say the same thing about Mom. And, I guess, about me.

I like Sixto a lot, more than Marilyn. He's in charge of overall strategy. Marilyn does mostly press relations, but it's not a big campaign staff. Everybody ends up doing a little bit of it all.

I gave Dad a kiss. Mom finally noticed that I was wearing Darlene's T-shirt.

"Where did you get that?" she asked.

"It's Darlene's," I answered.

"You look good, Lauren," said Sixto. "Very cute . . . very real-looking."

"Lauren's not real-*looking* . . . she's *real*," said Dad. Mom laughed. Sixto ruffled my hair, which is short and straight and doesn't look good when it's ruffled.

I tried to straighten it out.

The rally was as boring as I expected. I was the only kid there. The other candidates hadn't made their kids come along. I tried to listen to Mom's six-point speech about the city budget and schools, but my mind kept drifting.

My stomach growled. I was starving. The one thing I had learned already about politics was that *nothing* either started or ended on time. Everybody always has one last question. Adults act as if they're being graded on their participation at meetings. It's so dumb.

They really didn't need me at all. I just sat in the back of the room. I didn't even sit on the podium with Mom. I started daydreaming about getting so good at the bars that I beat Becky. Patrick was happy for me. He asked to take me to a special training camp so that I would get really good.

My father nudged me. I guess my eyes had started to close. I heard a round of applause. I clapped, too, just excited that it was finally over. Dad gave me a strange look. I looked up on stage and realized that I was cheering for Mom's opponent, the incumbent, Alvin Theodore. Doesn't that sound like the name of a jerk?

I was sitting in an area filled with Mom's supporters. Nobody else in my row was clapping. I put my hands over my mouth and pretended to cough.

Finally it was Mom's turn to speak. Mom's opponent had been on the city council for years. He doesn't believe in spending money, except on himself. He wears $600 suits and crocodile shoes. He doesn't even care that crocodiles are an endangered species. "All Alvin Theodore believes in is low property taxes," said Mom. "He doesn't care that low taxes have meant no money for our schools, for our elderly. No money to attract businesses and stores. He's a one-note politician, and it's time to change that note to a symphony."

I applauded even louder than before to make up for my mistake. At last the meeting was over.

"Okay, Lauren," whispered Dad. "It's time for us to go into our act." Dad and I hand out leaflets at these things. Sixto's taught me to try to shake people's hands and look them in the eye. "Everyone wants to see the children of the candidate," says Sixto. "And you're perfect for the part."

I didn't feel like playing my part tonight. "My hands hurt from my workout on the bars," I told Dad. "Do I have to shake hands?"

"Just give out the literature," said Dad. "And remember to smile."

I rolled my eyes and put on a fake smile. I went to the back of the auditorium, and I passed out the leaflets about Mom. Some people were really rude. They didn't want to take them, and they kind of brushed by me as if I were trying to sell them used comic books.

I was too tired to look into people's faces anymore. It had been a long day. I had gotten up early for school, then spent two hours at gymnastics, and now this boring rally. I just kind of pushed the leaflets in front of whoever passed by.

"I'll be glad to take one," said a familiar voice. I looked up, grinning.

"Patrick!" I exclaimed. "What are *you* doing here?"

"I wanted to hear your mom," said Patrick. "She was terrific."

"Mom, Dad!" I shouted, turning around. "Patrick's here!"

Mom and Dad were stuck in the middle of the aisle of the auditorium, surrounded by about twenty people. "They're busy," said Patrick. "You don't have to bother them. Tell your mom I thought her education plan sounded right on target."

"I will," I said. Patrick ruffled my hair. When Patrick did it, I liked it.

"And tell them for me that you were great in practice today," said Patrick.

I could feel myself blushing. "Excuse me," said a stranger. "May I have one of those leaflets?"

"Uh, sure," I stammered.

Patrick winked at me. "I'd better let you get back to work," he said. "I'll see you tomorrow."

"You bet," I said. Just then my stomach growled. I was so embarrassed. Right in front of Patrick, but he just laughed and leaned closer to me. "Watch it, tiger," he whispered. "You sound like you belong in the Denver Zoo."

"I'm starved," I admitted.

"Haven't you eaten since practice?" Patrick asked.

I shook my head no.

Patrick rummaged in his pocket and pulled out a package of Life Savers. "Here," he said. "This will hold you for at least a minute."

"Thanks," I said. "But I need pizza."

"Are your parents going to be long at this meeting?" asked Patrick, sounding really concerned. "I could take you for a slice."

"This is one of the few nights that Mom and Dad and I are eating together," I said. To tell the truth, I would much rather have gone for pizza with Patrick.

I watched Patrick's back. I couldn't believe he had taken the trouble to come to the meeting. I couldn't wait to tell Mom and Dad.

But of course, I had to wait. It took them a good fifteen minutes just to make it to the back of the auditorium. By that time, the place had practically emptied out, and my stomach was growling so loudly it sounded like it really did belong in the zoo. Why was it that Patrick cared that I was hungry, but Mom didn't? That's politics, I guess.

5

A Horrible Suggestion

Mom can be weird. One minute up onstage, she can look and sound as if she's the most energetic person in the world. Then, when she's alone, she loses it.

By the time we finally got to leave the rally, she was exhausted. Dad drove us home. I was glad Sixto wasn't coming back to our house for pizza. It's not that I don't like Sixto. It's just that I don't like him and the other campaign workers being around all the time.

Dad drove. I told him what a fantastic day I had in gymnastics. Mom leaned against the window with her eyes closed.

"That's terrific, honey, but wait and tell me about it when we get home," whispered Dad. "Your mom's catching forty winks."

"That's a stupid phrase," I said. I blinked my eyes up and down forty times. It didn't feel at all like sleeping. Dad watched me in the rearview mirror. "What are you doing, Lauren?" he asked.

"I'm catching forty winks," I said. Mom laughed.

"It didn't make any noise. How could it wake you?"

Mom smiled. "I wasn't really sleeping. I was just resting."

We pulled into the driveway of our town house. I got out and did a cartwheel on the lawn. Sometimes I just can't help myself. I like doing cartwheels at weird moments, and I had been cooped up at the dumb rally.

"Lauren," asked Mom, "can you help bring in some of those boxes? Then Dad can go for the pizza."

I looked down at my hands. They were grass-stained, and they were hurting me a little.

"I almost ripped my palms on the bars today," I said. "Do I have to?"

"Are you seriously hurt?" Mom asked. "I know that the bars can really tear up your hands."

"It's called a rip, Mom," I said. Mom never gets gymnastics jargon right. And she's always worried that I will get hurt doing gymnastics. I realized that it wouldn't be a good idea to make too big a deal about my hands.

"I'll do it," I said, going over to the car and pulling out one of the boxes. "Is our car going to be full of boxes forever?" I asked. "It seems like you're always taking boxes to the campaign headquarters . . . and bringing them home."

Dad laughed. "Lauren's got a point."

I picked up the box of literature. It was heavy. "I should get Patrick to give me extra credit for weight work while the campaign is going on," I said, as I schlepped the box into the living room.

Our living room looked like a campaign headquarters those days. Two months before, if I had kept my room as messy as the whole house was looking, Mom would have yelled at me.

I set the box on the floor. "Lauren, don't put it there, honey. I need it upstairs in my bedroom. Those are the briefing papers on toxic waste that I need to read before tomorrow."

"You mean I'm carrying toxic waste!" I shrieked, jumping away from the box.

"Of course not," Mom said with a sigh. "Those are papers *about* toxic waste."

"It was a joke, Mom," I said wearily. "Remember jokes?"

"I'm sorry, Lauren," said Mom. "Please take the box upstairs."

"I told you — my hands hurt," I whined.

Mom just looked at me. "If you're hurt, maybe you should think about taking a day off from gymnastics," said Mom.

"Forget that," I said quickly. I grabbed the box. "I do think you should write a note to Patrick telling him that I don't need to do push-ups. I'm getting all the upper body work I need lifting boxes for your campaign. Speaking of Patrick, did you see him at the meeting? He came! Isn't that terrific? He says that he's going to vote for you. I think that's so excellent — "

"Lauren, honey," said Mom, "just take the box upstairs."

I did what I was told. I hopped back down the stairs, taking them two at a time. Mom was in the kitchen on the phone, talking about the campaign, naturally.

I went to the fridge and got out some juice. Mom hung up the phone. She smiled at me.

"So how did you think the rally went this evening?" she asked.

"Patrick said he thought you were terrific."

"I didn't ask you what Patrick said. I asked what you thought."

"I thought it was cool that Patrick came," I said. "You know how hard he works. He was working with us all afternoon, and I bet he was tired, but he came anyway."

"Could we please have a sentence that doesn't have Patrick in it?" asked Mom.

"Well, all you want to talk about is the campaign," I mumbled. "Patrick is just as interesting. He wanted to take me out for pizza. Naturally I had to wait for you. I would rather have gone with Patrick."

"Lauren," said Mom, "we warned you from the beginning that this campaign would take up a lot of time for all of us, but I thought you realized how important it was." Mom's voice sounded tight, and I knew I had hurt her feelings by saying I'd rather have gone with Patrick.

"I'm sorry," I said quickly. "I didn't mean it, Mom. I think it's great that you're running, and I'm proud of you. I'm just tired. You know I had a full workout at gymnastics, and then when I was starving I had to go to the rally. I'll be better once Dad gets here with the pizza."

"I've been thinking," said Mom. "I realize that you're going to have so little free time during this campaign. Maybe it would be a good idea if you dropped gymnastics for a while."

I stared at her. "Is this your idea of a joke?"

Mom looked startled at the expression on my face. I was practically growling, and this time it wasn't my stomach. It was me.

"No, I'm not joking," said Mom. "I'm thinking of you. You have your schoolwork. This campaign is eating into all our free time together."

Luckily just then Dad came in with the pizza, so I didn't have a chance to blurt out to Mom how stupid her idea was. I was standing with my hands on my hips staring at her.

"Pizza delivery," Dad sang out. "Hot pizza."

"I don't want any," I grumbled.

Dad put the pizza down on the table. "What's going on?" he asked. "You were the one who was starving." Dad got out the plates.

"I think she's exhausted from gymnastics," said Mom.

"I am not!" I yelled.

"Lauren," said Dad, "don't talk to your mother in that tone of voice. She's tired, too!"

"I am not tired!" I hollered. "Mom is making this all up. She just wants me to quit gymnastics. I won't! I won't!"

Mom and Dad looked at each other. They gave

each other a look that I hate, the one that says, "See, I told you so!"

I wanted to run upstairs to my room, but I was afraid to. If I did, Mom and Dad might seriously make me quit gymnastics. I know my mom and dad. They pride themselves on being able to "talk things out" intelligently.

I heaved a big sigh and tried to control myself. I made myself sit down and take a piece of pizza even though I had completely lost my appetite. I stared at the cheese and picked at it.

"I'm sorry I yelled," I said quietly.

"I'm sorry I got you so upset," said Mom. I looked at her. At least she wasn't saying that it was all my fault. Mom continued. "I'm only think-ing about what's best for you," she said.

"Oh, sure," I said sarcastically. I couldn't help myself.

"What does *that* mean?" Mom asked.

"I *love* gymnastics. It's my whole life. You just want me to quit so I'll have more time to cam-paign for you."

"Lauren," said Dad, angrily, "you can't talk to your mother like that."

"I'm sorry," I muttered. I sighed. It had been one of the best days of my life at gymnastics, and now it was being ruined because all my parents could think about was Mom's dumb campaign.

"Wait a minute, Carl," said Mom. "Lauren's got a right to her opinion."

"I'm glad I've got *some* rights around here," I said.

Mom leaned across the table and put her hand on my arm. "Honey, of course you have rights — "

"Yeah, but you want me to quit gymnastics. I swear if you make me quit, I won't. I'll earn money somehow to pay for my own lessons. I'll bet Patrick will give me a scholarship. At least *he* likes me."

Dad cleared his throat. Dad is always the peacemaker in our house. I guess Mom and I are too much alike. We both look very calm on the outside, but we have a slow burn. When we get mad we find it hard to calm down.

"Lauren, you're getting worked up over nothing," said Dad.

"Nothing! Today I had the greatest day of my life at the gym, and now you want to take it all away from me."

"Nobody wants to take anything away from you," snapped Mom. She sounded as angry as I was. "I was just suggesting that there are going to be inordinate demands on all of our time, and gymnastics may be too much for you."

"What does 'inordinate' mean?" I asked. "You sound like you're giving a speech."

"It means excessive," said Mom, "which is the way you are about gymnastics. We're all going to be on a tight schedule with this campaign. I just think that the time we can spend alone will be precious."

"Yeah, like we're having so much fun now," I said.

Mom looked hurt and I felt bad. Sometimes I say things sarcastically that sound worse than I mean.

"I'm sorry you find being at home such a drag," said Mom.

"I don't, Mom," I said. "And I am proud of you. But, please, please, don't make me quit gymnastics."

"Lauren, you've always known that we don't think gymnastics should be the most important thing in your life," said Dad. "That's why I was worried about you getting so involved in the first place."

"It's not the most important thing in my life," I lied, even though I had just said the opposite.

"Maybe we should table this discussion until we finish eating," said Mom, taking another piece of pizza.

"I can't eat if I'm worried that you're going to make me quit," I said. I was telling the truth. My stomach felt as if it were tied up in knots.

"Let's see how things go," said Mom. "I was just suggesting that you drop out for a little while."

"You can't drop out of gymnastics for a little while. All the other Pinecones will get better than me, and they'll get ahead. I have to work like mad now just to keep up with Cindi," I whined. "I'd have to go back to the baby group. Don't you know anything about gymnastics?"

Dad looked at me over his piece of pizza. "Lauren, that's exactly the kind of tone of voice that makes us think gymnastics is too much for you."

I made a face. They had me in a double bind. If I yelled and told them how unfair they were being, I'd be told that I couldn't continue gymnastics.

"Look," I said, trying to keep my voice calm. "I know I can be a good campaigner and do gymnastics."

"What about your schoolwork?" asked Dad.

"No problem," I said.

"Well, let's take Mom's advice and drop this subject for now," said Dad. "If later on we find that it's too much for you, we'll discuss it again as reasonable people, okay?"

Mom tried to smile at me. "We only want what's best for you," she said.

I hate those words: "We only want what's best for you"! Adults say that when they want to get their own way. I knew if I opened my mouth again, I'd be in trouble. So I stuffed it with pizza. Sometimes eating is the best way to end an argument. At least that's always been true at our house.

6

Trying Too Hard

I woke up feeling tired the next day. I didn't dare tell my folks I felt crummy because I knew my mom might say, "Why don't you skip gymnastics?" No way.

I made it through my classes at school without falling asleep. When I got to the gym, Patrick announced that we'd be working on our tumbling today. Normally I like tumbling, but tumbling takes the most out of me, and I only like to do it when I have a lot of strength.

First we worked on something called a back walkover to a split. It looks very dramatic, because one moment you are doing a backbend to a handstand, and the next your legs are split wide on the floor.

39

"It takes control," said Patrick. "There is no preliminary landing on one foot before the split. You shift your weight immediately to the right hand while you're still in the handstand for the walkover."

"I don't get it," I admitted. Sometimes when Patrick explains things in words, it's hard to picture it.

"Here," said Patrick, "hold my clipboard for me. I'll show you."

"I'll hold it," said Ashley, but Patrick handed it to me. I smirked at Ashley. Patrick bent backwards, kicked his legs, and went effortlessly into a perfect handstand.

"Now, I'm not as flexible as you girls," said Patrick. Patrick can hold a handstand forever, and his voice sounds just as strong when he's upside down in the middle of a handstand as it does when he's right side up.

Patrick split his legs in the air as if he were starting a back walkover, but instead of putting his feet back down, he leaned over on his right hand and slid into a split.

"Wow!" I said. I was cradling Patrick's clipboard in my arms.

Ashley giggled.

"What are you laughing at, twerp?" Jodi asked.

"Lauren," whispered Ashley. "She looks so silly holding Patrick's clipboard like she's in love with it."

Jodi glanced at me. I blushed and put the clipboard under my arm, trying to look very professional.

Jodi laughed. I gave her a dirty look. She shrugged her shoulders. "Lighten up," she whispered to me. "I hate to agree with Ashley, but you looked like an ad for a movie: *Crush on the Coach*."

"*Crush on a Clipboard*," giggled Cindi.

I gave *her* a dirty look, too. "I do *not* have a crush on Patrick," I whispered, "or his stupid clipboard."

"Your nose is growing, Pinocchio," whispered Cindi.

"Are you calling me a liar?"

Cindi's eyes widened. "Lauren, it's me . . . Cindi. I was just teasing. Sorry. Can't you take a joke?"

"Not today," I admitted.

"Girls," said Patrick, "I'm not doing this for my health. Will you please stop whispering? Do you get it now?"

"Lauren gets it," teased Ashley. "She gets everything you say."

"Good," said Patrick. He got up from his split.

"Come on, Lauren, you try it now. Once you've shifted the weight to your right hand, get your left hand out of the way so your forward leg can shoot through for the split."

I pointed my right foot to start the backbend that would lead to the walkover. I bent over in a backbend and split my legs in the air. I tried to put all my weight on my right hand, but I wasn't strong enough to hold it. I ended up falling hard on the mats on my hip.

"That's okay," said Patrick. "You've got the idea."

"But I didn't do it," I grumbled.

"You will next time," said Patrick.

Ashley did it nearly perfectly. So did Cindi.

I felt like a failure. I stood in line behind Darlene. "It's not as easy as it looks, is it?" she asked.

I shook my head. "Nothing is as easy as it looks," I grunted.

Darlene made a face. "You're in a great mood today," she said sarcastically.

"Don't mess with me," I warned her.

"I was just going to ask if anything was wrong," said Darlene.

"Sorry," I muttered.

Patrick signaled to Darlene that it was her turn. Darlene is really flexible, and when she moved from the handstand down into the split she did it in one fluid motion.

"Beautiful!" said Patrick. He grinned at Darlene. "Let's be sure to work that into your routine."

Naturally I fouled it up on my second try. "Don't worry," said Patrick. "You'll get it." He turned to the rest of the Pinecones. "Okay, that's enough of that. Let's work on your front flying somersaults. Help me make a hill." I groaned to myself. Front flying somersaults are something I can't do yet. It's a somersault done in the air. From a standing position you hurl yourself through space with enough spring to tuck around into a somersault in the air. None of the Pinecones are ready for it, but we're learning the fundamentals.

We piled up the thick mats one on top of the other until they formed a mound almost three feet high.

"Gravity will do most of the work for you," said Patrick. "Start to tuck only after you've completed a jump straight up in the air. The trick is not to tuck your head to your chest until you've completed the jump. I'll spot you. Lauren, you first."

"Why me?" I whined.

"Just because," said Patrick.

I climbed on top of the mats. "Come on," said Patrick. "We've tried this before. You can do it."

I took a deep breath and jumped, but I could feel Patrick really struggling to hold me up as I tucked into the somersault position and tried to throw myself through the air.

"No, no," said Patrick. "You're trying too hard."

Ashley giggled. "Lauren always tries too hard," she said.

I gave her a dirty look.

"Don't worry, Lauren. You'll get this move in time," said Patrick.

"Time," I muttered. "Who knows if I'll have time. . . ."

"What does that mean?" asked Darlene.

"Nothing," I snapped, thinking about my mom telling me that I should quit gymnastics. If she had seen me working out that day she would have proof that she was right. Luckily Patrick doesn't let parents watch our workouts.

This was one of the few afternoons at gymnastics that I was genuinely glad would be over. But it wasn't over yet.

Becky's a Beast — Baca's the Best

Becky and her group joined us for the cool-downs. We stretched out on the mats. All the Pinecones had noticed that I was in a lousy mood, but Becky hadn't seen me all day. Not that it would have mattered. But maybe she would have thought twice about starting a fight.

"Take deep breaths," said Patrick in a soothing voice. He believes in something called "creative rest." We lie on the floor and visualize ourselves doing a trick perfectly that we've practiced all day.

I was so tired that all I could see were red streaks behind my eyeballs. I tried to imagine myself doing the flying somersault. Eventually we were supposed to be able to spring from the floor into a tucked position without the help of the hill of mats. I couldn't even fantasize doing it from the hill.

"Okay, girls," said Patrick. "That's it for the day."

"My creative rest wasn't very creative today," I admitted. Patrick laughed. That made me feel better. I love to make him laugh. I think it made Becky jealous. Because she's the best gymnast, she hates it when Patrick pays attention to anybody else. And I do think he wants me to do well. Patrick grinned at me and went over to talk to Jodi's mom.

Becky turned on me. "I'd like to put you into permanent creative rest," she said.

"Becky, you've got such a wonderful way with words," I taunted. "It's amazing your brain has room for all of them. Maybe you should give up gymnastics and do something more creative."

Jodi giggled.

That just made Becky madder. "My brain isn't cluttered up with stupid political slogans. 'Baca's the Best.' They forgot a letter. It should read 'Baca's a Beast.' "

"At least I've got *something* on my brain, airhead," I muttered to Becky. If I hadn't been in such a stupid mood, I would have said some-

46

thing wittier, but I shouldn't have baited Becky. She's only trouble.

"Ha!" said Becky. "If your mother is half as lamebrained as you are, I wouldn't vote for her."

"Leave my mother out of this," I snapped.

Becky tossed her long blonde hair out of her eyes. She has a way of doing it that is very annoying. "All politicians are sleazy, anyhow," she said.

I put my hands on my hips. "My mother is not sleazy," I yelled, a little louder than I intended.

Patrick turned around. "What's going on?" he asked.

"Becky called Lauren's mom sleazy," chirped Ti An. I wished she had kept her mouth shut, although I knew Ti An thought she was being loyal.

"Yeah," said Jodi. "She said 'Baca's a Beast.' She can't say that about Lauren's mom."

"I was saying that about Lauren," said Becky in a haughty voice.

Patrick looked annoyed. "Becky, did you really call Lauren's mother sleazy? If you did, I want you to apologize right now!"

"I said *all* politicians are sleazy. Not just her mother. It's the truth. That's what my dad says."

"He's wrong," said Cindi, sounding very angry. "Tell her, Patrick."

I couldn't complain that my friends weren't loyal.

"I admire Julia Baca," said Patrick.

"She's a politician," muttered Becky.

"Becky, you're way out of line," warned Patrick. "It's too easy to say that you hate all politicians. At least Lauren and her mother are out there doing something."

Becky glared at me. Her dirty looks are of professional quality. I mean, she looked vicious.

Patrick walked back across the floor to continue his conversation with Jodi's mom.

"I still say Baca's a beast," Becky taunted me.

I couldn't think of a clever retort. "*You're* the beast" was the best I could do.

Jodi came to my rescue. "Yeah, Becky's a beast and Baca's the best."

I grinned.

"Pinecones for Baca!" chimed in Cindi.

"Pinecones for Baca! Pinecones for Baca!" Soon all the Pinecones were chanting it. Even Ashley was mouthing it quietly.

"What does that mean?!" demanded Becky. "It's stupid."

"Is not!" said Jodi.

"Is too!" said Becky.

"Is not!" shouted Jodi. "Pinecones for Baca! Pinecones for Baca!"

"This is a great political discussion," I smirked. "We sound like two-year-olds."

"I think 'Pinecones for Baca' has a great ring to it," said Patrick with a grin, coming across the floor with his clipboard in his hand. He hadn't heard what had come before.

"I thought you said you didn't want politics in the gym," I said.

"Well, I didn't," said Patrick. "But I have a feeling things aren't under my control."

"Is that my fault?" I asked guiltily.

"Pinecones for Baca! Pinecones for Baca!" Jodi continued to shout.

Patrick winked at me. "You've got to admit, it's a great slogan," he said.

We went into the locker room with Jodi still leading the chant: "Pinecones for Baca! Pinecones for Baca!"

Becky put her hands over her ears and tried to escape. Patrick was right. "Pinecones for Baca" had a nice ring to it, just because it seemed to make Becky want to throw up.

After we marched into the locker room, I thought that would be the end of it, but I was wrong. The Pinecones had only begun.

"I think we should get T-shirts that say 'Pinecones for Baca,' " said Jodi.

"That's a terrific idea," said Darlene.

"That's the most stupid idea I've ever heard," said Becky. "You'll walk around the city wearing T-shirts that say 'Pinecones for Baca' and nobody will know what it means."

"That's the point," argued Jodi. "People will stop us on the street and ask about it, and we can explain why Julia Baca is the best candidate. Lauren, don't you think it's a great idea?"

To tell the truth I wasn't so hot for it. "Pinecones for Baca" was a nice one-time chant, but if I never heard it again I wouldn't mind. Scratch that. I wouldn't mind hearing "Pinecones for Baca" if they were cheering *me* for winning a medal at a gymnastics meet. But I liked the idea of keeping my gymnastics and Mom's campaign completely separate. As far as I was concerned, they could pass a constitutional amendment: No politics in the gym.

"Come on, Lauren," urged Jodi. "I'll bet your mom would love us going around with Pinecones for Baca T-shirts."

"Oh, sure," I muttered sarcastically. "I'll bet that's just what Sixto would want to spend money on."

"Who's Sixto?" asked Darlene.

"Mom's campaign manager. He watches every penny."

"You mean the campaign would pay for them?"

asked Jodi. Once Jodi gets an idea into her head, she goes for it.

"Jodi's idea *is* kind of cute," said Cindi. "People would stop us and ask us what it meant. We could give them a spiel about your mom. Maybe we should go to campaign headquarters and tell them."

"I've never been to a campaign headquarters," said Ti An. "I told my teacher that the mother of my friend was running for city council, and she said if I wrote a report on it I could get extra credit."

"Great," I mumbled. "That's one way to win the third-grade vote."

"It's worth a shot," said Darlene.

"I vote we take Jodi's idea to campaign head-quarters," said Cindi.

"I still think that's the stupidest idea I've ever heard," said Becky.

That did it. I couldn't let Becky have the last word.

"You don't know anything about campaigning," I said. "Come on, guys, follow me to headquarters."

8

A Cute Angle

Mom's campaign headquarters was within walking distance of the gym. I don't know why Marilyn turned up her nose at Patrick's gym. Patrick's gym looks like a luxury box at Mile High Stadium compared with Mom's campaign headquarters. It's on the second story over a delicatessen, and it always smells like pickles.

It's really just one room, about the size of a big classroom, with a lot of folding tables and chairs and telephones everywhere, sometimes four to a desk. There's a little partition in the back, where Mom and Sixto sometimes go for privacy.

There were a couple of volunteers on the phone, but it didn't look like the center of the universe. Sixto was sitting on top of one of the tables, his legs dangling over the side, a portable telephone to his ear. Mom jokes that Sixto would look naked without a telephone. Sixto waved at me.

"Who's that?" whispered Jodi.

"That's Sixto — Mom's campaign manager," I said.

"Where's your mom?" Darlene asked.

I looked up at a big board on the wall. It's weird to be able to find out where your mom is by looking at a giant schedule, but every day Sixto lists Mom's schedule up there so that all the volunteers know where she is.

"She's at a fund-raising tea," I said, "but she's supposed to be back here soon."

"Wow!" said Ti An. "I didn't know a campaign headquarters would be so neat!"

I stared at her. "What's neat about this place? It's a dump." I was right. The place was even messier than our house: full of newspapers and those darned leaflets.

"I don't know," said Ti An. "It just looks like a fun place. I like it!"

"I know exactly what Ti An means," said Darlene. "Somehow it looks like a grown-ups' hangout."

Sixto put down the phone. He was all smiles.

"Hi, Lauren," he said. "To what do we owe the honor of this visit? Are these volunteers you recruited?"

"No," I said quickly. "This is my team. . . ."

Just then, Mom came in the door, followed by Marilyn and a couple of volunteers. "I hate pleading for money," Mom was saying to Marilyn in a loud voice.

"Careful," said Sixto. "We may have some big contributors here. Lauren's brought her gang."

"Hi, Mom," I said. "You know all the Pinecones." Mom smiled. She shook hands with everyone, just as if she were campaigning.

"I wish eleven-year-olds had the vote," said Jodi. "I'd vote for you."

"Thanks, Jodi," said Mom. "I could use your help. You can help Lauren pass out leaflets any day — that is, if you're not too busy with gymnastics."

I hated that line, "not too busy with gymnastics." It seemed like Mom's little dig at me — a reminder of our discussion the night before.

"We're here because we've got a great idea," said Jodi. "For the campaign. Pinecones for Baca — "

"Julia," interrupted Marilyn, "we've got to go over our notes from the meeting."

Mom looked distracted. "I'm sorry, Jodi . . . you know, I'm busy."

"Come on, guys," I said quickly. "They're really too busy around here for us. . . ."

"Wait a minute," said Sixto. "What's a Pine-cone?"

"It's the name of our team," I said snootily.

"What kind of a team?" he asked. "You're not a basketball team, are you?"

"Gymnastics," I said. I sighed. Didn't Sixto know anything about me?

"Julia, you didn't tell me Lauren was a gymnast."

"We're the Pinecones," said Jodi, not afraid of finding an opening now that Sixto was listening to us. "And we want to get T-shirts that say 'Pine-cones for Baca.' "

"People won't know what it means," explained Cindi, "but when they stop us, we'll tell them they should vote for Julia Baca."

Sixto was stroking his chin. "Gymnasts, huh," he said. He looked at me. "Lauren, what can you do?"

"Do?" I asked.

"You know," said Sixto, impatiently. "Can you walk on your hands?"

I giggled.

"Come on, Lauren," urged Ti An. "Show him what you can do."

"I'm in a skirt," I complained.

"You've got tights on," said Cindi. Cindi and Darlene cleared a space for me by shoving the tables back. I felt so embarrassed.

"What should I do?" I asked.

"Do the back walkover split we were practicing," said Darlene. "That looks impressive."

I kicked into a handstand with my legs split into the air, but I couldn't hold it. I was afraid to try coming down in a split, so I just righted myself into a normal back walkover.

Nobody but the Pinecones knew I hadn't done the trick. Sixto and Marilyn and the other campaign workers applauded as if I were Mary Lou Retton. I took a bow, but I could feel that my face was bright red.

"Can all you kids do things like that?" asked Sixto.

"Oh, sure," said Jodi. "Watch!" Jodi took off and did a roundoff. It's a cartwheel with a half-twist turn at the end. It's real easy, but it looks impressive.

One by one, the Pinecones put on a mini-show. Cindi did a handstand pirouette.

Ti An did a perfect front walkover.

All the campaign workers seemed to think it was neat, everybody except Mom. She had her arms crossed against her chest. She was trying to look patient, but I thought her smile seemed pasted-on.

"Uh, hey, guys," I said, "we'd better get out of here. They have work to do. . . ."

"No . . . no," said Sixto. "I like this. Everybody identifies your mom with school and education. People think she's a little too much the intellectual."

"You know," added Marilyn, "these kids are a natural for TV. They're all very photogenic."

"That's just what I was thinking," said Sixto.

Mom just stood there, looking annoyed. "I don't want you exploiting Lauren," she warned.

"It's not exploiting," said Sixto excitedly. "We can just use a few shots of them caterwauling — "

"It's cartwheeling," I said.

"Whatever," said Sixto. "It's a great lead-in to show Julia's concern for the total welfare of all children. You're not just the education candidate. It'll show that you love sports and that you and your family aren't just eggheads. It's eggsactly what we need."

"We're going to be on TV!" shouted Ti An.

"Not so fast," I said. I looked at Mom. She did not look happy. But nothing could stop Sixto's enthusiasm. He was a match for Jodi.

"You like the idea, don't you, Lauren?" said Sixto, paying more attention to me than he ever had before.

I tried to stop myself from grinning too widely. What could be better! Mom wanted me to quit gymnastics because it interfered with the campaign, and now her own campaign manager wanted to use my gymnastics. Talk about sweet revenge.

I scrunched up my mouth. I didn't want to seem too eager. That would be out of character. "Well," I drawled, "if it will help the campaign . . ."

"Julia, you've got to admit, it's a cute angle," said Sixto. "We can use it on the TV ads we're planning for the end of the campaign. What did you kids call yourselves again?"

"Pinecones for Baca!" I said.

Mom looked at me. The one thing I've got to say for Mom is that she's not dumb. "It's a cute angle, all right," she said. Then she shook her head. "If it's all right with Lauren, it's all right with me."

"Yippee!" said Ashley. "We're going to be on TV."

I looked at her. " 'Yippee?' " I said. "Nobody says 'yippee.' "

But inside I was shouting "Yippee" myself. No way could Mom talk about me quitting gymnastics now. My gymnastics was part of the campaign.

9

Trapped

A couple of weeks went by. The campaign was rushing into high gear. "When are they going to use the Pinecones for Baca idea?" complained Jodi in the locker room before class. "I thought they loved it, especially that guy, Sixes."

"Sixto," I laughed. "Well, they've been busy. You can't expect everything to stop just for gymnastics. I'm just grateful you guys got Mom off my back. She hasn't mentioned me quitting gymnastics since you came to the office."

"Why would you quit gymnastics?" asked Darlene.

"I don't want to worry you guys, but Mom was making threatening noises that maybe I should quit because the campaign was taking up so much of our time. . . . What a joke!"

"But it didn't happen," said Jodi.

"Thanks to you," I said. "When we went over to campaign headquarters, Mom couldn't say anything again. And she hasn't!"

"Hey, you sound really angry," said Cindi. Darlene just looked at me.

"Wouldn't you be angry?" I demanded.

"Yeah, but your mom didn't push it. She's got a lot on her plate right now," said Cindi. "I'd cool it."

"I have," I said defensively. I was not exactly sure why I felt so defensive.

We walked into the gym. "Hey, Lauren!" shouted Ashley. "Look what I'm wearing." Ashley was wearing a bright yellow T-shirt with my mom's face on the top of a pinecone.

"Where did you get that?" I asked. Ashley pointed. I looked over toward the door of the gym. Sixto was standing in the doorway, surrounded by gymnasts. A guy with a video camera was behind him, and kids were pushing and shoving, trying to get their pictures taken.

Sixto was passing out T-shirts left and right.

"Hey!" I shouted, as I saw him handing one to Becky's friend Gloria. "You're not a Pinecone."

I pushed my way through the crowd. I was out

of breath by the time I got to Sixto. "What are you doing?!" I yelled at him.

"I've got the T-shirts," said Sixto. "They look great. We're going to shoot the commercial."

Becky slipped one of the T-shirts over her leotard.

"You're doing it all wrong!" I shouted at Sixto. "Everybody isn't a Pinecone. The Pinecones are the intermediate group. You gave them out to beginners and to advanced kids. It's all wrong!"

Sixto stared at me as if I were speaking some weird language. "Don't worry about it," he said.

"But . . . " I wailed. Jodi pushed to the front of the line. "Neat-o!" she shouted as she grabbed one of the T-shirts. I took one from Sixto. In huge black letters it read, "JUMPING FOR JULIA!"

"It's supposed to say 'Pinecones for Baca!' " I said.

"It does," said Darlene, pointing to some small letters underneath the pinecone.

"This isn't what we had in mind," I complained.

Darlene held up her T-shirt. "I think I need an extra large," she said. "Then I can knot it."

"But it's all wrong!" I repeated.

"I like yellow," said Darlene.

"He's giving them to everybody," I hissed. Darlene put on her T-shirt.

Suddenly Patrick came down from his office. "What's going on here?" he demanded.

Sixto stuck out his hand. "Hi, I'm Sixto Ulloa. I'm Julia Baca's campaign manager. The kids came up with the idea for a TV commercial showing them all jumping for Julia. We thought we'd shoot it today."

"We didn't say anything about jumping for Julia," I complained. "It was just supposed to be the Pinecones for Baca."

Patrick looked terribly confused. "Noboby told me anything about a TV commercial," he said. He looked at the T-shirts. "Those are kind of cute," he said, "but — "

"It's simple," said Sixto. "I just need to shoot a few minutes of the girls jumping."

"Wait a minute," said Patrick. "We're about to start a gymnastics class. You can't interrupt everything."

"But, Patrick, it's for Lauren's mom," said Becky sweetly. She did a pirouette as if she were modeling the T-shirt.

"We've *got* to do it, Patrick," said Jodi excitedly. "It would be un-American not to vote with our cartwheels."

"I like that," said Sixto. "You can say that in front of the camera."

Patrick held up his hand. "Hold it! This is a

gymnastics club, not a TV studio. I'm all for Julia Baca, and I'm happy to help her out, but you've got to give me some notice. *And* give me a chance to find out what Lauren wants. This is her club, not her mother's."

"That's telling him, Patrick," I said.

Sixto looked at me. Sixto is used to getting what he wants when he wants it.

"Don't you want to make the commercial?" complained Jodi. "We can all be stars."

"Yeah," said Ti An. "This is going to be so neat!"

"My mom's not running for President," I shouted. "It's just for the dumb city council."

"Don't film that," said Sixto quickly. "Film the kid who wanted to vote doing caterwauls."

"Cartwheels!" I yelled.

"Lauren," said Patrick, "calm down!"

But I couldn't. I *hated*, just *hated* having *my* gym invaded by Mom's campaign. Who cared about Pinecones for Baca?

Becky caught the eye of the cameraman. When she was sure he was looking at her, she took off down the mats and did two perfect back flips.

The cameraman taped Becky. "Wonderful!" Sixto said. He turned to the cameraman. "Are you sure you got that?" he sounded worried.

"Maybe we should have her do it again."

"She's not even a Pinecone!" I screamed at Sixto.

Cindi put her hand over my shoulder. "Lauren, relax," she said. "It's not the end of the world." She had on her yellow Pinecones for Baca T-shirt over her leotard.

"Do you want Becky in my mother's commercial?" I hissed.

I couldn't take it anymore. I went over to Sixto and tried to get his attention, but he was in the middle of saying something to Patrick. I started hammering on his back with my fists. "It can only be Pinecones!" I screamed at him.

Sixto and Patrick stared down at me as if I had completely lost it. The cameraman finally lowered his camera.

"What's wrong with her?" Sixto asked Patrick.

"Lauren," said Patrick, "go to the parents' lounge and get a drink of water. I'll meet you there."

He sounded stern, almost angry. I had tears in my eyes. I was out of control. Now even Patrick thought I was a dork.

"Wait," argued Cindi, tyring to stick up for me. "It was Becky's fault for taking a T-shirt."

"I didn't do anything wrong," whined Becky, all innocence.

"Cindi, stay out of this!" snapped Patrick. "Lauren, go!"

The rest of the Pinecones stared at me. I had no choice. I turned and left. If I could have sunk through the floor, I would have been happy. But there were no trapdoors. It was just me who was trapped.

10

If I Had a Daughter . . .

The parents' lounge is opposite the locker room, and it's completely sealed off from the gym. All the furniture in the parents' lounge looks like rejects from a college dorm. The couches sag a little, and some of the caning on the rocking chair is a little stringy. The walls are decorated with posters from old Olympics. It's not very glamorous, but it's comfy. It's got a refrigerator with an automatic ice maker for all our injuries, and a VCR for us to watch gymnastics tapes.

Patrick wanted a place where our parents could wait for us and be comfortable, but not where they could look in on the gym. Patrick knows that parents can make kids crazy. Parents are welcome to relax in the lounge and wait for us, but he doesn't want them staring at us.

I've always liked that, but now I wished there were just one tiny window so I could see what was going on in the gym. I wondered if they were going to film the entire commercial without me. That would be great. Pinecones for Baca. . . . Everybody except the one kid with the name Baca. It would be a political embarrassment.

I got myself a glass of cold water and flopped down on one of the old corduroy couches.

The door opened and Patrick walked in. I half stood up.

"Sit down," said Patrick. I couldn't tell how mad he was.

Patrick walked to the refrigerator and put some ice in a glass. He got some water. It seemed to take forever. He turned to face me, leaning against the counter by the refrigerator. He took a sip of water, still not saying anything.

I licked my lips. "I'm sorry I yelled so much out there," I said.

"You can yell, but you can't hit," said Patrick. "You know that, Lauren. It's one of the first rules of the gym."

"I didn't hit another gymnast. . . . I was just trying to get Sixto's attention."

Patrick frowned at me. He didn't have to say anything.

"I hit him," I admitted. "I guess I have to go out there and apologize."

"He's gone," said Patrick. "I told him that he'd have to come back and shoot the commercial another day. I can't have people interrupting our class without warning."

"All right, Patrick!" I shouted, pumping my right arm in the air. "You're the only one who doesn't think the whole world should stop for the campaign."

"It's not all right, Lauren," said Patrick. "You still owe that man an apology. I hated to see you out of control like that."

"So the whole world knows now that I'm not the perfect candidate's daughter. So what? Six-to's always telling Mom I'm just 'perfect' for the campaign. I get good grades. I always do what I'm told. Well, now he knows the real me."

"Lauren . . . I can imagine that it's not easy to be in the middle of the campaign, but just remember one thing. . . ."

"I know what you're going to say," I said with a sigh. "I should be proud that my mom is running for office. She's a great person. It's going to be good for the city of Denver if she wins. Alvin

Theodore's got to go. I'm lucky to have her for a mother. . . . I know, I know." I felt like I was giving a campaign speech.

"That's *not* what I was going to say," said Patrick. "Will you let me finish my own sentence?"

"Sorry," I said. "It's just that I know you're right. I *am* proud of Mom . . . and — "

"Lauren," interrupted Patrick, "let me talk for a second. I was going to say that your problem with being the perfect candidate's daughter, as you say, is that you really are as terrific as you seem. If I had a daughter, I'd want her to be just like you. Feisty, a fighter, yet kind and smart. Face it, Lauren. It's a proven fact, you're just a terrific kid."

Of all the things I expected Patrick to say to me, that was the last. I must have looked as shocked as I felt.

"But . . . but. . . ."

Patrick just smiled. "Sometimes for a bright, articulate kid, you do have trouble getting the words out."

I had to blink back tears. "How come I'm crying when you're being so nice to me?" I sniffed.

"Come on, champ," said Patrick. "Let's go back into the gym. I've got an idea for the commercial for your mom that will make the real Pinecones for Baca look terrific."

"You're not furious with me for getting so mad at Sixto?"

"I told you that I think you should apologize to that man. You were wrong to yell, but he was partly to blame for the disturbance. Sixto apologized to me for not giving me notice. After gymnastics, go to headquarters and apologize. You'll say you're sorry and that'll be the end of it. Don't you want to know my idea for the commercial?"

"What is it?" I asked.

"A real Baca for the top," said Patrick.

I stared at him, not understanding, but all I could hear were the words Patrick had said before. "If I had a daughter, I'd want her to be just like you. . . ."

11

Pinecones Crash
for Baca

We walked back into the gym. "Go warm up with the others," said Patrick.

"Did Patrick yell at you?" Jodi asked me as I lay down beside her on the mats to warm up.

I just smiled, thinking about what Patrick had said to me. I couldn't help myself; I started grinning.

"One thing about Lauren," said Cindi. "She's like the weather. Stick around long enough and her mood will change."

I giggled.

Patrick clapped his hands for our attention. We all sat up on the mats. "Okay, kids. Listen up. You all know that they want to make a commercial for Lauren's mom. My idea is that we form a pyramid with Lauren on the top. Lauren will do a flying somersault from the top of the pyramid."

"I can't do a flying somersault," I argued.

"It'll be just the same as doing it from the hill of mats, like we did awhile ago."

"Lauren couldn't really do it then, either," piped up Ashley. "*I* could. I'm little enough to be on the top of the pyramid."

"I can do it without a hill to help me," bragged Becky. "I can do it standing on the mats. I don't need to be on top of the pyramid. That'll look better."

"You were the one who said my mother was sleazy," I told her.

"I said *all* politicians, not your mother."

"My mother is a politician. And the T-shirts say Pinecones for Baca."

"Only in tiny print," argued Becky. "Besides, I can be a Pinecone for this occasion. I've got the T-shirt."

"Girls, stop arguing," said Patrick. "Becky, if you want to campaign for Lauren's mom, that's terrific, but the pyramid will just be for Pinecones. After all, it was Jodi's idea. She gets to be the center of the pyramid. Bottom layer, Jodi."

"Great," joked Jodi. "I come up with a great

idea and I get to hold up a pyramid."

"Let's try it," said Patrick. "Jodi, Darlene, and Cindi, get on all fours on the mats. You three are the strongest. Brace yourselves."

Patrick helped Ti An and Ashley scramble onto the backs of Jodi, Darlene, and Cindi. Ashley and Ti An crouched on all fours, too.

"We're too little to hold up Lauren," whined Ashley.

"Don't be ridiculous," said Patrick. "The two of you are plenty strong to hold up little Lauren."

"Little Lauren better get up there fast!" grunted Cindi.

Patrick lifted me on top. "Stand with one leg on Ashley and one on Ti An," said Patrick. "You don't have to hold it very long."

"That's good," I said, " 'cause Ashley's got a bony back."

"Hurry," grunted Darlene from the bottom of the pyramid.

Patrick held me with his hand along the small of my back.

"Okay, Lauren, jump for the somersault. I'll spot you around."

I raised my hands over my head but before I could jump, the pyramid collapsed beneath me.

I crashed into Ti An, who tumbled down between Jodi and Darlene.

Becky gave one sarcastic clap. "That'll look great on TV. 'Pinecones crash for Baca.' "

"Shut up," I said. "Let's try it again."

"Easy for you to say," grumbled Jodi. "You're on the top."

"Did I hurt you?" I asked worriedly.

Jodi shook her head. "Am I or am I not the originator of the Pinecones for Baca slogan?"

"I don't think you knew how much trouble it would cause," said Darlene as she got back down on all fours to form the base of the pyramid.

I was worried. What if the Pinecones didn't like the idea of my being on top? One great thing about the Pinecones was that we were all equal. "Hey, guys," I said. "Maybe we should forget the whole thing."

Patrick shook his head. "No way, Lauren. You're in this campaign whether you like it or not. You might as well have some fun with it."

"Are we sure this is fun?" I asked.

The Pinecones all nodded. "If we're willing to be at the bottom of the pyramid, you've got a responsibility to be on the top," said Darlene.

She sounded so serious. "I'm not running for office myself, you know," I said.

"Maybe someday," said Cindi.

"No way," I said.

Cindi and Jodi got back down on their hands

and knees with Darlene to form the base of the triangle.

This time when I stood on top it didn't collapse underneath me. I can't say I did a great somersault from the top, but at least I managed to get my knees tucked. With Patrick's help I got around.

"Do you think it'll be okay for the commercial?" I asked Patrick. "I can't really do it without you spotting me."

"Sure you can," said Patrick. "Let's try it again."

The Pinecones grunted. But this time when I got on top of the pyramid I almost made it around in the somersault by myself.

"When are they coming back to do the commercial?" I asked Patrick.

"Tomorrow," he said.

"You mean, that's all the time I get to practice?" I wailed.

"It'll be okay," said Patrick. "I talked to the person making the commercial. They don't want it to look perfect."

"That's one thing they don't have to worry about," said Becky.

The trouble was that I had to agree with her.

12

Why Does That Sound Like a Threat?

I walked over to Mom's campaign headquarters after practice. I knew Patrick was right. I had to apologize to Sixto in person. If I went home to dinner and Sixto had already told Mom how I had been, I'd be in deep trouble.

The campaign was in its final few weeks, and headquarters was getting more and more crowded. It's hard to believe how many folding tables and chairs can fit into one room.

Most of the campaign workers knew who I was, even the ones I didn't know. It's strange when everybody knows your name and you don't remember theirs. I'm not saying that all adults look alike, but when I have to meet so many of them, I forget their names.

I got away with mumbling "Hi" as I made my way to the back of the room, where Mom was talking to Sixto and Marilyn. Sixto had his back to me, and Mom spotted me first. She waved to me and gave me a big smile. I was pretty sure that Sixto hadn't had a chance to tell her how I had behaved. She wouldn't have been smiling at me if he had talked to her already.

Sixto turned and gave me a smile as if nothing had happened. He was in the middle of a story about the campaign. I shifted nervously from one foot to the other, waiting for him to finish so I could get my apology over with.

"So Theodore is speaking to a group of retirees at a senior citizens' center," said Sixto, "and he's got all the media there because he's touted it as a big event. He's giving his usual baloney about how Julia Baca will spend all their money on the young. Their taxes will go up . . . blah . . . blah. . . .

"Then this old biddy interrupts him and asks everyone who's got a grandchild or a great-grandchild to raise their hands . . . and then she gives a speech for *you*. The TV cameras are loving her. . . . She'll be on all the news shows tonight

. . . I'll bet my life on it. Theodore looked like he wanted to strangle her, and of course the TV cameras got all of that, too."

"Was she an African American?" I asked.

Sixto raised his eyebrows. "How did you know?" he asked.

" 'Cause it sounds just like GeeGee," I said.

"Who's GeeGee?" Sixto asked.

"She's the great-grandmother of Darlene, one of the Pinecones," I said.

Mom smiled at me. "Darlene's one of Lauren's best friends. Her dad is 'Big Beef' Broderick of the Broncos."

"Darlene is a *real* Pinecone," I said.

Sixto clapped me on the back. "You mean we're going to have Big Beef's daughter in our ad? Maybe we could get this GeeGee to let us tape her for our own commercial. This could be good."

Sixto was so involved in thinking about the commercial, he seemed to have totally forgotten that just one hour ago I had been hammering on his back with my fists. I had to interrupt him. I coughed. "Uh, Sixto," I stammered, "I came to talk to you about how I acted today. I'm sorry I lost my temper."

Sixto waved his hand in the air. "Forget it," he said. "I talked to your coach. He sounds like

79

a smart cookie. He said he'd work out something that will be cute. We're coming tomorrow. Julia, now's the time to hit back at Theodore with our plan for the elderly. . . ."

I couldn't believe it. Sixto really didn't care that I had lost my cool and screamed at him. I had to say one thing for political campaigns. Things moved so fast that there wasn't time for me to get in trouble.

Mom wasn't quite so easily distracted as Sixto. She interrupted him. "Wait a minute. What's this about Lauren losing her temper?"

"Oh, it's nothing, Mom," I said airily. "You go on talking to Sixto. I've got to work on my part for the commercial."

Mom frowned. "Sixto . . . I'm not as convinced as you are that this commercial with the gymnasts is a good idea."

Sixto shook his head. "It's a winner. Believe me. I went over today and checked the place out. It'll be good. We need to show you in a loose environment, and believe me, that place is loosey-goosey."

I wished Sixto would keep his mouth shut. "Loosey-goosey" is not a compliment in Mom's book.

But nothing can stop Sixto when he's on a roll.

"I liked that place," said Sixto. "Lauren almost pounded me into the dust 'cause I was giving the wrong kids T-shirts, but that gym has great visuals."

"Uh . . . 'pounded into dust' is just a figure of speech," I said quickly.

Mom looked at me suspiciously. "Sixto," she said, "I want to talk with Lauren alone."

"Mom," I complained, "you've got things to do."

"Lauren," warned Mom. I bit my lip. I knew that tone of voice. It wasn't the candidate speaking anymore. It was Mom.

Mom took me behind one of the partitions. "Okay, Lauren, what exactly went on this afternoon?"

"Sixto said it was no big deal," I tried.

"I know you," said Mom. "You wouldn't have come over here to apologize to Sixto unless you had felt you had done something seriously wrong."

I couldn't believe it. I was getting into trouble for taking the trouble to apologize to Sixto.

"It was Sixto's fault," I argued. "He came in with the T-shirts, and he started giving them out left and right. I mean, it wasn't *really* his fault. He just didn't know who was a Pinecone and who wasn't. So maybe I raised my voice a little to tell him that he was doing it wrong."

Mom wasn't fooled. "Raised your voice a little? And for that you felt you had to come all the way over here to say you were sorry?"

"Well, you know the gym can get a little noisy. Maybe I had to scream a little to get Sixto's attention." I squirmed. I didn't want to have to tell Mom that I had pummeled Sixto with my fists and that Patrick had made me go to the lounge to cool down.

Mom picked up a pencil and started tapping it on the desk, always a bad sign. "I know, Lauren, that this campaign's been tough on you. You've been wonderful, but I don't want you to feel that you have to do too much."

"I'm not doing too much," I said quickly.

"I think that maybe this commercial is too much. You don't have to do this commercial. In fact, I don't think it's a good idea."

"Mom, I want to," I said. I thought about all the hard work the Pinecones had done, letting me stand on top of the pyramid.

"Think about it, Lauren," said Mom. "I know you love gymnastics, and it's been the one place where my campaign hasn't intruded."

I swallowed hard. Sometimes I forget that Mom's as smart about me as she is.

"I didn't know you knew I felt like that," I said.

"Why do you think I didn't pursue our discussion a while back about you quitting gymnastics because it was too much for you?"

"I just thought you kind of got too busy with the campaign and forgot about it."

Mom gave me a long look. "I haven't been so preoccupied that I forget what my daughter's like. That's why I'm not sure about this commercial."

"But all the Pinecones *want* to do the commercial. I want to do it. We want to help on your campaign."

"You can help more by leafleting and going canvassing."

"Mom!" I yelled. "You've got to let us do this commercial." I couldn't believe it! Life was just turning topsy-turvy. Suddenly I was the one who had to fight to get gymnastics into the campaign instead of keeping Mom out of it. But I knew the Pinecones would hate me if Mom canceled the commercial.

"Mom!" I wailed. "You're being so unfair!"

Mom sighed. "Shh," she said, pointing to the partition that didn't go all the way up to the ceiling. I suppose everybody was listening to us. If you're the candidate's daughter, you're not allowed to call your mother unfair.

Sixto knocked on the partition. "Excuse me, Julia. But we've really got to get you going. You're giving a speech in five minutes."

Mom looked at me. "All right, Lauren," she said. "We'll go ahead with the commercial, but I want no more outbursts from you. Remember now, this was your idea."

Now why did that sound so much like a threat?

13

That's Not Show Business — It's Politics

The next day Darlene cornered me in the locker room. She sounded all excited. "Did you know that GeeGee taped a commercial last night for your mom?" she asked. "Just like we're doing."

"You're kidding!" I said. "Boy, they work fast."

"Someone called her yesterday afternoon," said Darlene. "She said she loved doing it."

"You mean we have to compete with Darlene's great-grandmother?" asked Cindi. All the Pinecones know that GeeGee is quite a character.

"Maybe Barking Barney will put me in one of his commercials," said Jodi, pulling on her Pinecones for Baca T-shirt.

Cindi pointed to the corner. Becky was preening in the mirror, and she had on her Pinecones for Baca T-shirt, too.

Becky saw us staring at her and quickly left the locker room. "We'd better get out there quick," said Cindi, "before she steals the show."

We rushed out into the gym. Patrick was conferring with Sixto and Mom.

Sixto had come with a bigger film crew, including a couple of people with lights. It was turning out to be a much bigger deal than it had seemed yesterday.

Sixto waved to me. I went up to him and Patrick. I liked that they were including me in the plans as if I were a grown-up. "We decided that as long as we're doing this we might as well make it look good," said Sixto.

Patrick turned to Mom. "I've just got to tell you again how thrilled I am that I live in your district so I can vote for you," he said. "And I want you to know what a terrific kid you've got in Lauren. She really is a joy to work with."

Mom shook Patrick's hand warmly. "Well, she certainly thinks the world of you," she said.

I grinned. Maybe today would go better than I thought. I liked Mom and Patrick shaking hands.

So did Sixto. "Excuse me," he said to Patrick.

"Can you say that again so we can get it on tape?"

"Sure," said Patrick, but he looked embarrassed. "Lauren's a joy to work with."

"No, no," said Sixto. "Just shake Julia's hand and tell her you want to vote for her. You're very photogenic."

"I think they should have kept in the part about Patrick saying you're a joy," Jodi whispered to me as we watched the cameraman tape Patrick and Mom. They both looked kind of phony compared to the first time when Patrick had come up to Mom spontaneously.

"Okay, kids," shouted Sixto. "We have to do this quickly. We're taping Julia all over town today."

I noticed the cameraman watching Becky, who was practicing a spectacular routine on the uneven bars. Of course, she just happened to be wearing the bright yellow Pinecones for Baca T-shirt over her leotard. The cameraman whispered something to Sixto. Sixto nodded.

"We'd like to shoot that girl on the bars," he said.

Patrick looked at Becky. "Why don't you use Lauren?" he said.

"Good idea," said Sixto. "Lauren, can you do what that girl just did?"

Becky was doing a giant circle around the high bar. "Uh, not exactly," I said as I watched her do a flyaway dismount, something I couldn't do in a million years.

"Show them your new release move," said Patrick. "Come on, I'll spot you."

"We didn't practice for them to tape this," I whispered.

"No problem," said Patrick. "I'll be there to spot you."

I took a deep breath and went over to the chalk bin. "Go for it, Lauren," shouted Cindi.

The cameraman was right in my face as I stuck my hands in the chalk. He moved even closer. I took a step back and tipped over the entire chalk bin, dumping it all over my Pinecones for Baca T-shirt.

Mom rushed in to try to dust me off. I was so embarrassed, and the stupid cameraman never stopped taping. I could hear Becky laughing in the background.

Patrick stood under the uneven bars, shaking his head. "Come on, sport," he said. "This isn't a meet. Nobody's scoring you."

I grabbed hold of the lower bar and did a glide kip mount, but my kip was very jerky, and Patrick had to put his hand under my back to shovel me up to the bar.

I would have done better if I hadn't been so nervous, but when I tried to swing to the high bar I missed it completely. The camera caught me landing like a fish on the lower bar, swinging on my stomach. I slipped off and fell on my back.

Mom rushed in again, scared that I had really hurt myself. I picked myself up.

"I'm fine, Mom," I said through gritted teeth. I started to grab the lower bar to remount, but Sixto was waving at the cameraman, pointing to Becky, who was over on the floor mats. She just happened to be practicing her back flips. She did a spectacular roundoff to back flip, flying high into the air. She landed it perfectly, with her arms stretched out high above her in a victory pose with the "Jumping for Julia" logo front and center. The cameraman ran over there, and Becky repeated the same move, picture-perfect.

"Don't worry about her, Lauren," said Patrick, patting me on the back. "Come on, let's set up the pyramid."

"*Real* Pinecones out on the mats," I shouted. Becky gave a sly look and stepped off the floor mats. She was still smiling for the cameraman.

"If they only knew her real personality," muttered Cindi. The cameraman zeroed in on us. Cindi started giggling. Jodi elbowed her way in, exaggerating her movements for the cameras. Darlene was in the corner trying to fix her hair.

"Come on, Darlene!" shouted Jodi. "Nobody's going to see your face."

The cameraman swung around to shoot Darlene sticking out her tongue at Jodi.

"You're going to love this," Patrick said to Sixto and my mother as Jodi, Cindi, and Darlene started to form the pyramid.

"You can't see the T-shirt logo," complained Sixto.

"Wait," said Patrick. He helped Ashley and Ti An kneel on the backs of Cindi, Darlene, and Jodi.

"Hurry, Lauren," said Jodi. The pyramid already looked shaky. Cindi giggled nervously again.

Patrick lifted me up by the armpits and put me on top. I stood up.

Ashley's back was really swaying. I could hardly hold my balance.

Suddenly my foot slipped off Ashley's back. I tried to catch myself and grabbed hold of Ti An's shoulder.

She squealed and dived nose-first into Jodi. We collapsed into a heap on the mat, giggling uncontrollably in front of the cameras.

Patrick stood over us shaking his head. "Okay.

Now that we've got the nervousness out of the way, let's do it again for real," he said.

Sixto looked at his watch. He and the cameraman whispered together. "Thanks. We've got all we need," said Sixto.

"Wait," I yelled. "We didn't do it!"

"It's okay, Lauren," said Sixto. "I loved what we got. We're just going to use a few seconds of this."

"We're late, honey," said Mom, giving me a kiss. "Thanks a million. You kids were terrific."

"But . . . but," I stammered.

Sixto patted me on the back. "Don't worry, Lauren, we've got great stuff," he said. I glared at him. I hate to be patronized. But Sixto didn't notice my glare, nor did Mom. The crew packed up the videotape equipment, and they were out of the gym in record time.

"That's it?!" asked Darlene from the bottom of the pile.

Patrick looked as bewildered as the rest of us. "Sorry, guys. I guess that's show business."

"It's not show business. It's politics," I muttered angrily.

"I think it was kind of neat," said Becky as she pulled off her Pinecones for Baca T-shirt.

She threw it on a bench. "I don't need this anymore," she said.

"If they use Becky and not us, I'll kill myself," I said to the Pinecones.

"If they use Becky and not us, we'll kill you," said Jodi cheerfully.

I laughed. Jodi's a great joker; at least, I *think* she was joking.

14

Let Me Out Of Here

Two days later Mom greeted me with a big smile at breakfast. "The commercial is ready!" she said. "I just got off the phone with Sixto. He says it's terrific!"

"How could it be finished already?" I asked.

"The magic of videotape. You know how fast things happen in a campaign. Sometimes we do a new commercial overnight. Sixto wanted to show it this morning, but I told him he had to wait until all the Pinecones could see it. Why don't the Pinecones come over to headquarters after practice? We'll wait for you until five o'clock."

"Thanks, Mom!" I said. "That's cool. The Pinecones are going to be so excited."

"I'm glad we've finally found something about this campaign that makes you happy," said Dad.

Mom and I just looked at each other. "We've worked that out," I said quickly. "Right, Mom?"

"Right," said Mom. "We'll see you at five."

When I told Patrick and the Pinecones that the commercial was ready, they couldn't believe it!

"That fast!" exclaimed Patrick.

"They have to do it that fast in politics," I told Patrick. "Sometimes they do a new commercial overnight," I said, trying to sound like an expert.

"What time are they going to show the commercial?" asked Becky.

"Hey," said Cindi. "Why would you want to go? It's just sleazy politics."

"Maybe I've gotten interested," said Becky. "I might want to volunteer for Lauren's mom."

The other Pinecones looked at me, but I didn't know what to say. I couldn't really turn down any potential volunteers, but I knew Becky didn't give a hoot about Mom's campaign. She just wanted to see if they had used her in the commercial.

I couldn't think of any graceful way to keep her away.

After practice, Patrick drove us all over to headquarters in his minivan. If Patrick was surprised that Becky was coming along, he didn't let on. But I got to sit up front next to him.

When we got to headquarters Mom and Sixto were standing over a TV set in the corner. "Is this the screening?" asked Becky. "Where's the big screen?"

"It's just a video," I said disgustedly. I ran up to Mom. "Have you seen it yet?" I whispered to her nervously as Sixto ordered a group of campaign workers to get up and give Patrick and the Pinecones some of the folding chairs around the TV.

Mom nodded, but she looked distracted. Maybe she still didn't like the idea of having gymnasts invade her campaign.

I settled down in front of the TV screen while Sixto slipped the videotape into the VCR. The commercial opened with Mom shaking hands with a lot of different voters all over the district. Then it showed Patrick and Mom shaking hands and Patrick saying that he was proud to vote for my mom.

"Julia Baca's daughter is a straight-A student and a kid who flips out for sports," said the voice-over, "even if she's not the best." Just then the camera caught me with chalk dust all over myself.

"Julia Baca is the champion of all kids, not just her own."

The camera showed Becky doing giant circles on the bar. Then it showed her doing her superb back flip.

Suddenly the commercial switched to scenes of Mom at the senior citizens' center, talking to a large group of people. The camera zeroed in on Darlene's grandmother.

"There's GeeGee!" shouted Darlene.

"Old people care about kids," said GeeGee. "That's why I'm voting for Julia Baca!"

"Young and old flip for Baca," said the voice-over, "because she doesn't care just about champions. . . . She's there for all the kids . . . on the top and on the bottom." Then the commercial ended with me tumbling down from the pyramid and all the Pinecones giggling in a heap.

I could hardly breathe, I was so angry. I wanted to put my fist through the TV screen. I looked around at the Pinecones. They seemed to feel as miserable as I did. We had come across as idiots. Cindi was still staring at the blank TV screen. Jodi was biting her fingernails. Ti An just looked at the floor.

Patrick wouldn't look at me or my mother. He stared out the window, his arms across his chest.

"I think it's a winner," said Sixto. "It shows Julia's human side, and it's got humor. We can only afford to use it on cable, but I'm going to show it to the news shows. I bet they pick up a piece of it."

"It's humiliating!" I wailed. "I look like the worst klutz in the world."

"The camera doesn't lie," whispered Becky.

I ignored her. "You made us all look terrible," I yelled at Sixto.

"You look cute," said Sixto.

"Cute!" I yelled.

"I think I looked great," said Becky.

That was the last straw. I couldn't take it. "You stink!" I shouted.

"Lauren," Mom warned, "control yourself."

"No way!" I yelled. I jumped out of my seat and ran between the folding chairs toward the door.

"Lauren," said Patrick, "wait!"

"Hey, Lauren!" I heard Cindi yell.

I heard my mom yelling for me to stop.

I heard Patrick shouting for me to stop.

But I didn't stop. I couldn't. I didn't know where I was going. I just had to get out of there!

15

A Stubborn Block

I ran. I guess you could call me a runaway.

I ran around a corner and stopped. Now what? I've never been the kind of kid who runs out of the house, even when I was little. The one time I threatened to run away, I let my mom help me pack, and I told her I needed her help crossing streets. She walked me to the corner and talked me into coming back home for some ice cream. But that had been when I was only six years old.

This was much worse. When I was six, I thought humiliation would go away. I had a shorter memory. Now my humiliation was about to be broadcast to the world. I couldn't stand it.

I wondered if anybody was following me. I stopped under the awning of a shoe store. I pretended to be window shopping and walked sideways to the corner, hugging the glass of the showroom.

I looked around the corner. Cindi was leading the pack of the Pinecones.

"Lauren! Lauren!" Cindi yelled. It was so embarrassing. I ducked into the shoe store.

"Can I help you?" asked the saleswoman.

"I'm just looking," I gasped. I was still out of breath. I noticed that I had stopped in front of a display of three-inch heels. The saleswoman looked at me suspiciously. It's awful how some people are always suspicious of kids. It's as if the fact that we're shorter than adults means that we're all shoplifters or something.

I slunk out of the shoe store. I looked around the corner. I didn't see any of the Pinecones. They must have either gone back to Mom's headquarters or were looking up another street.

I crossed the street. At least now I was old enough to do that myself. I didn't know where to go or what to do. No wonder I had never run away before. It's hard to decide what to do.

I felt a little foolish but kind of stubborn at the same time. I wanted Mom to worry. I looked up.

I was close to the library. I went inside. It's the one place where a kid can go and they don't ask you any questions about why you are there alone.

It's a modern building made out of red bricks and wooden beams. It's not too big; not like the main library in downtown Denver. The children's room is on the ground floor in the back, facing the mountains.

The librarian didn't pay any attention to me. That's why I like libraries. I went and got a magazine and put it in front of me, but I couldn't read. I stared out the window for the longest time. I knew I should call home or call Mom at headquarters. I knew at the very least I should call Cindi or Darlene or Jodi and tell them not to worry. But I didn't want to.

It was like I had a stubborn block in my body that felt pretty solid. I *knew* what was the right thing to do, but I didn't want to do it. Maybe that's what happens to real runaways.

Everything that had happened was my fault. I knew that was the truth. Deep down I couldn't even blame Mom. I wanted to blame her, but I couldn't. She might have wanted me to quit gymnastics, but she hadn't pushed it.

She had known that making the commercial with the Pinecones was a mistake. She had given me a chance to back out, but I had insisted.

So now what could I do? I had embarrassed Patrick. I had embarrassed my team. Soon everyone would watch me look like the world's klutziest gymnast, and I didn't have anybody to blame but myself.

Someone tapped me on the shoulder. I jumped a mile high. I think I expected it to be Patrick, but it was the librarian. He pointed to the clock.

"It's seven o'clock," he said. "We're closing."

I couldn't believe I had sat there for two hours. Now Mom and Dad would be really furious that I hadn't called them. Even Patrick would be mad.

"Did you hear me?" asked the librarian. He didn't really sound mad. Maybe he thought I had a hearing impairment.

I nodded. I put the magazine back on the rack. It's strange to try and act normal when you don't feel normal. I've spent lots and lots of time in libraries and I've never thought anyone was staring at me, but now I did.

I walked outside. It was getting dark. I knew I was in serious trouble if I didn't go back to campaign headquarters. I should at least call Cindi. She was my best friend.

But the stubborn block hadn't disappeared. I didn't *want* to see my mother. I didn't *want* to call Cindi. If I called Cindi, she'd have to tell her parents where I was and they would have to call my mother.

I knew I wasn't really going to run away. I just wasn't going home yet. I couldn't.

I kept walking. Without really thinking about it, I realized where I was going. I was walking toward the gym.

I knew it would be empty and locked up, but it was the only place I wanted to be.

16

Splintering

The light over the Evergreen Gymnastics Academy sign was shining. I wondered if Patrick kept it on all night. There are no windows facing the street, and except for the light shining up toward the sign, the gym looked deserted and depressing.

I hunched up my shoulders as a cool wind blew the sign. It creaked like the uneven bars creak when we're doing our exercises, but except for that lonely noise, the street was quiet and silent.

I huddled in the doorway with my back to the door. I knew I couldn't stay there. I'd have to go home soon.

Suddenly the door fell back behind me. I stumbled and tripped. Patrick stood holding the door, staring down at me.

"Come in here," he said. He sounded grim.

I followed him into the parents' lounge. "How did you know I'd show up here?" I asked.

"I didn't," said Patrick. "We looked all over for you. Your father's at home. Your mother is hoping you'll come back to the campaign headquarters. Cindi and the other Pinecones were sure you'd call Cindi's house. I said I'd come back here, just in case you tried to call me."

"All that and I've only been missing two hours," I tried to joke. "I hope it's not on the news. It'll be bad for the campaign."

"This isn't funny, Lauren," said Patrick. Patrick reached for the phone next to the refrigerator.

"Please, wait. Don't call them," I begged.

"I have to," said Patrick.

I sank down onto one of the couches. It was so hard to believe it was on this very couch that Patrick had once told me I was a joy to work with. Now I bet he hated me for causing so much trouble.

I heard Patrick ask for my mother on the phone. "She's here," he said. "I don't know. . . . I called you as soon as I found her." Patrick cupped his hand over the receiver. "Where were you?"

"I went to the library," I said.

Patrick almost laughed. "We never thought to look there," he said. "She went to the library." He turned to me. "Your mother wants to talk to you," he said.

I shook my head.

Patrick held the receiver out to me. I shook my head even more fiercely.

Patrick sighed and put the phone back up to his ear. "Let me talk to Lauren. I'll bring her home in half an hour."

Patrick hung up the phone and leaned back against the counter. "Your mother will call your dad, and Cindi and her parents and the other Pinecones, and let them know you've been found. You know you *have* to go home," he said.

"I know," I muttered. I picked at one of the tufts around the button on the couch. "Do you want to adopt me?" I asked. "You said you wanted a daughter like me."

"You already have two parents who love you," said Patrick.

I curled my legs up underneath me. The stubborn block in my chest hadn't disappeared. "They should adopt Becky. It looks like she's their daughter anyway on that commercial."

"Lauren, you shouldn't have run out of campaign headquarters. And you certainly shouldn't have stayed away all that time. You knew people would be worried."

"I know that," I grunted.

"Why did you?" asked Patrick.

I didn't answer him for a long time. Finally I said, "What did you think of that commercial?"

Patrick walked over to the refrigerator and took out some apple juice. "Do you want some?" he asked.

"You're avoiding the question," I said. "What did you think of that commercial?"

"I'm not a media expert," said Patrick.

"You're a voter," I said.

"I thought Darlene's grandmother was very convincing," said Patrick. "I liked the way they used her to show that your mother cares about all people."

"What about the gymnastics part?" I asked.

Patrick rubbed the back of his neck. "I didn't like the way it made fun of you . . . but — "

"See!" I interrupted. "I'm not going home until they pull that commercial."

"Lauren, don't be ridiculous. You can't use that as an excuse to run away."

"Did you know my mother suggested that I

quit gymnastics because her stupid campaign was taking up so much of our time?"

"I didn't," admitted Patrick. "But you haven't quit gymnastics. How come?"

"I told her I wouldn't," I said stubbornly.

"And . . . ?" said Patrick.

"And what?" I demanded. "That was all there was to it." But I knew where Patrick was going with this conversation and it made me uncomfortable.

"And why haven't you quit?" Patrick asked.

"Mom backed down," I said.

"Do you know why?" Patrick asked.

"Because she knew I loved gymnastics more than anything else in the world," I argued. "She had to back down."

"Your mom didn't back down," said Patrick. "She made a decision to let you stay in gymnastics because she not only loves you, she also respects you."

"Yeah, that's why she let them shoot a commercial that makes a fool out of me."

"That might have been a mistake," said Patrick. "But parents are human. They make mistakes."

"She was worried before," I mumbled.

"Before what?" asked Patrick.

I blinked. I wanted to cry. "I talked her into

letting us make a commercial. She thought maybe I should keep your gym and her politics separate."

Patrick sighed. "Well, life doesn't come in neat packages," he said. "We all make mistakes."

"I made the biggest," I said.

Patrick shook his head. "No, you didn't. You were trying to help your mom, and that was good. I like your whole family. I get lots of parents who are athletes themselves, and they want their kids to be involved in sports. But I admire your parents more than most."

"Oh, please," I begged, "don't tell me again how proud you are to vote for Mom."

"This has got nothing to do with your mom as a politician. But neither of your parents loves sports. They don't know anything about gymnastics and yet they don't stand in your way. They pay for your lessons, and I know your parents aren't rich. They just know it's important to you, and they trust you enough and love you enough to let you go for it."

The word "trust" killed me. I wondered if Mom and Dad would ever trust me again. I felt the stubborn block of wood splintering, but the splinters hurt. I blinked. I was having trouble not crying.

"Are you ready to go home?" Patrick asked me.

17

Something in the Eyes

If Patrick's gym had looked forlorn except for the light bulb hanging over the evergreen, our house was lit up like a Christmas tree. Every light was on, upstairs and down.

Patrick pulled into the driveway. I was hunched down in the bucket seat of his van. I looked up at the light over the door to our town house.

"I'll bet Sixto and everybody is in there," I muttered. I made no move to open the door.

Patrick didn't answer me. "Let's go," he said.

"Will you stay?" I begged. "And help me explain — "

"Lauren, no," said Patrick. "This is between

you and your parents. You've got to talk to them."

"I'd rather talk to you," I said.

Patrick smiled at me. "Thanks, Lauren. But I'm just your coach."

I thought about the kids teasing me about having a crush on Patrick. I did, but it didn't really help. I had to face my parents. I climbed out of the van.

The door to the town house opened. Mom came charging down the driveway. She hugged me without saying anything for a second. I knew that wouldn't last very long.

"Thanks, Patrick," she said.

Patrick nodded. "She's fine," he said.

I turned my head to look at Patrick as he got back into the van. I felt as if I were being abandoned. Mom had her arm around my shoulders.

Dad was standing in the doorway. He moved aside to let me and Mom in. I looked around the living room. It was empty.

"Where's Sixto?" I asked.

"He's not here," said Mom.

"Aren't you supposed to be somewhere tonight?" I asked sarcastically.

Mom looked so hurt that for a second I thought she was going to cry. "I've canceled everything for tonight. You just ran off without a word. You had to know we were worried. You've never done that before."

"I was only gone two hours," I whined. "Other kids run away for days."

"Lauren," warned Dad.

He was right. I knew I was on the wrong track.

"I'm sorry, Mom," I said.

"We were worried about you," said Mom.

"I can't believe you just went to the library," said Dad. "We went to Darlene's house, Cindi's house, Jodi's. . . . We never thought of looking at the library."

"I stayed there till it closed. It closes at seven. Maybe when you're elected to the city council you can get more funds for the library."

"Lauren, this isn't a joke about the campaign. I was so upset when you ran out like that!"

"Let's keep things in perspective, though, Julia," said Dad. He had a slight smile on his face. "As runaways go, we can't complain too much about Lauren. She went to the library and came home — all in under three hours."

"I know," said Mom. "But you didn't see her at my campaign headquarters. She ran out like a wild child."

"Well, I was upset!" I cried. "You let them make a commercial that makes fun of me and the Pinecones. I couldn't stand it! And then I knew you would blame me because you didn't want the Pinecones in the commercial in the first place . . . and — "

"I hated that commercial," said Mom. "I pulled it. I — "

"Huh?!" I interrupted. I couldn't believe what Mom was saying.

"You ran away before I could say anything. I told Sixto they had to change it."

"But why?" I blurted out.

"Are you kidding?" asked Mom. "I won't have a commercial for my campaign that stars Becky!"

I started laughing. I couldn't help myself. Mom began laughing, too.

"This really isn't funny," she tried to say.

"I know," I admitted. "Did you really tell them that they couldn't use the commercial?"

Mom nodded. "They want to reshoot tomorrow. They love the stuff with Darlene's grandmother, and it works well with the gymnastics. But we can skip it altogether if you'd rather. That commercial has already caused more than its share of problems."

"It's me who's been the problem," I admitted. "Not the commercial."

Mom smiled. "Not entirely," she said.

"Not entirely, what?" I asked.

"It's not entirely you who's been the problem," she said. "There's always Becky."

"Mom," I exclaimed. "You're too much! I never knew you realized Becky was such a pain in the neck."

"Well, she reminds me of somebody," said Mom.

"Who?"

"Alvin Theodore," said Mom. I giggled, thinking about Mom's opponent's bald head.

"They don't look anything alike," I said.

"I know," said Mom. "But it's something in the eyes. They both think they're better than everybody else."

"There's something else they have in common," I said.

"What's that?" asked Mom.

"They can be beaten," I said. "The real Pinecones for Baca have just begun to fight."

I called all the Pinecones one by one and told them I was okay, everything was okay, and they had to be sure to wear their Pinecones for Baca T-shirts tomorrow.

"You mean you aren't even in trouble?" asked Cindi.

"I just went to the library," I said.

I heard Cindi chuckle. "You have all the luck," she said. "Whoever heard of running away to the library?"

"I'm sorry I ran out on you."

"Don't do it again," said Cindi. "I hated it."

I blinked. I was going to cry again. "I'm really sorry," I said.

"Tell me again, why are we doing it over?"

"My mom wouldn't let them use Becky," I said. I started to giggle. "She says Becky reminds her of Alvin Theodore."

"Baca's the best," said Cindi.

18

They Finally
Got It Right

"I don't understand why they're reshooting it," complained Becky when the cameraman showed up at the gym.

Cindi just grinned at her. Naturally Becky had left her T-shirt at home.

"Sorry, Becky. I think they found that your face dissolved the videotape," said Jodi.

"That's not funny," said Becky. "This just confirms what I always thought. Politics is stupid!"

Becky went off into a corner to pout.

"Okay, girls," said Sixto. "Let's make this quick. We just need the pyramid."

Darlene, Jodi, and Cindi got into their places on the mats. Ashley and Ti An got on top of them.

I climbed onto their backs. Patrick stood behind me. "What if I foul up again?" I asked.

"Don't even think about it," grunted Cindi from the bottom.

"She's right," said Patrick.

The cameraman zoomed in on my T-shirt.

"Go, Lauren!" said Patrick.

I swung my arms down and then over my head. I bent my arms, trying to remember to keep my back straight. I went high into the air before I dipped my chin. I tucked my legs to my chest. My momentum turned me around. I was doing a somersault in the air, and Patrick hadn't needed to spot me.

I landed in front of the pyramid. I spread my arms in a huge V, showing off my Pinecones for Baca T-shirt.

"That's a take!" shouted Sixto.

The rest of the Pinecones cheered as the pyramid stood up.

"Atta girl, Lauren!" shouted Jodi, giving me a high five. The cameraman was still filming.

I looked over at Becky. She was standing next to Patrick. I guess she had tried to get in the picture after all. It didn't matter. This time it was the Pinecones, and this time it was for real.

"We're going to cut this and have the commercial on the air by four o'clock tomorrow," said

Sixto. "It's just the fresh look we need to finish out the week."

The next afternoon Mom showed up by herself at Patrick's gym. She had a videotape in her hand.

"Sorry to interrupt," she said to Patrick. "I'll wait till after practice if you want, but I thought the Pinecones would want to see this as soon as possible."

"There are *some* interruptions I don't mind," said Patrick. "We can show it in the parents' lounge."

Patrick told all the Pinecones to follow him to the lounge. I walked next to Mom.

"Shouldn't you be campaigning?" I asked her.

"I've got meetings all this evening," she said. "But I wanted to show this to you myself."

Patrick put the tape into the machine. We all sat cross-legged on the floor.

I watched closely. Instead of Becky doing giant circles on the bars, in the middle of the commercial there was a quick shot of the Pinecones beginning to form the pyramid.

Then the commercial cut back to the senior citizens' center. But at the very end, the voice-over said, "Young and old flip for Baca. Because she doesn't care just about champions . . . she's there for all the kids." The camera showed me doing a great somersault down from the pyramid!

The screen dissolved to black and then the words "Baca's the Best!" flashed on the screen.

"They finally got it right," said Mom, giving me a hug. Cindi just gave me a big grin.

"Let's watch it again," said Cindi. "I think I spotted Becky's ear in the corner. It was this strange red color."

I laughed so hard I thought I'd split my gut. But we watched the commercial again, and sure enough, I'm pretty sure it was Becky's red ear in the corner of the screen.

19

Patrick's the Best

The final week of the campaign went by in a blur. Every day after gymnastics, all the Pinecones hurried over to Mom's campaign headquarters. We did whatever we could — a lot of the time it was just running downstairs to the deli for food. I think everybody connected with the campaign survived on fast food that week.

The last weekend we went around door-to-door in the neighborhood, urging everyone to vote for Julia Baca. Everybody knew us. Our commercial had been on the air several times a day. We were the Pinecones, and people recognized our T-shirts.

Mom invited all the Pinecones and Patrick to come to the election-night party.

"What if we lose?" I asked.

"We're still going to have a party," said Mom. "If I win I want to thank everybody who worked so hard for me. And if I lose, I'll just try harder the next time."

I gulped.

"You mean, even if you lose, you're going to do this again?" I asked.

"Did you quit gymnastics the first time you took a nasty fall?" asked Mom.

"Maybe you won't lose," I said hopefully.

"The polls show it very close," said Mom.

"How can people vote for someone named Alvin?" I wondered.

"They have for twelve years," said Mom.

"It's time for a change," I said.

"Now, where have I heard that before?" said Mom.

I was a wreck on election night. The deli downstairs was catering the party, and I couldn't even look at food. That's not like me at all.

Headquarters had never been so crowded. Everybody even remotely connected with the campaign came to wait for the results.

"It's a good sign that so many people are here," said Darlene.

"Do you think so?" I asked anxiously. I was willing to believe in any omens.

Darlene nodded. "People wouldn't want to be around a loser," she said.

Patrick was in a corner talking to my dad. I looked at them together, and I thought about what Patrick had told me the night that I ran away. I had two parents who loved me. Win or lose.

Mom and Sixto were behind the partition on the phone.

Suddenly we all heard a whoop come from behind the wall. "Maravillosa!" shouted Sixto in his loudest voice.

The conversation stopped dead.

Sixto and Mom came out from behind the partition. Mom waved at me. I waved back. Mom shook her head. "Come up here," she mouthed. "Get your dad."

I went over to Dad and Patrick. "Mom says we're supposed to go up front," I said to Dad.

"Good luck, Bacas," said Patrick.

"You know," said Dad, as we made our way through the crowd, "that young man is very intelligent."

"You're just saying that 'cause you know he voted for Mom," I teased, but I loved it that Dad was learning to respect Patrick.

We reached Mom. "Do you have the results?" I asked her. She winked at me. Then behind her back she made a V with the first two fingers of her right hand. She turned so that Dad and I could see.

"You won!" I yelped, but before I could hug her, Sixto had gone to the microphone.

"Ladies and gentlemen," shouted Sixto, "the polls have closed, and they are already projecting a winner."

"It *is* time for a change!" I shouted at Sixto. I put my arms around Mom's waist and waved to the crowd.

"Baca's the Best! Baca's the Best!" the crowd began to chant, and Patrick and the Pinecones were leading the chant.

I didn't think I was going to cry on the night my mom won her first election, but I did. If Patrick had told me when the campaign started that I'd be crying tears of joy, I would never have believed him.

Cindi pushed through the crowd and gave me a hug. I started to cry even harder. Darlene and Jodi thumped me on the back. Ti An snuck in underneath. Even Ashley was grinning. But I couldn't stop crying.

Patrick moved in and took me aside. "Why am I crying?" I asked. I tried to laugh. "When I see people I love I can't stop crying."

"It's a proven fact that tears of joy are good for you," said Patrick with a smile.

I wiped away my tears with the sleeve of my Pinecones for Baca T-shirt. All around us, people were cheering "Baca's the Best!"

"You know what else?" Patrick whispered into my ear.

I shook my head.

"Both Bacas are the best," said Patrick.

No wonder I have a crush on my coach. Who wouldn't? The whole world may not know it, but Patrick's the best, too.

About the Author

Elizabeth Levy decided that the only way she could write about gymnastics was to try it herself. Besides taking classes she is involved with a group of young gymnasts near her home in New York City, and enjoys following their progress.

Elizabeth Levy's other Apple Paperbacks are *A Different Twist*, *The Computer That Said Steal Me*, and all the other books in THE GYMNASTS series.

She likes visiting schools to give talks and meet her readers. Kids love her presentation's opening. Why? "I start with a cartwheel!" says Levy. "At least I try to."